A STAGE FOR ROM

Nancy Faulkner

Wildside Press

ACKNOWLEDGMENT

It is a pleasure to acknowledge with thanks the help given me in the preparation of this book by Williamsburg Restoration Incorporated. I am especially grateful to J. Van MacNair, who smoothed the research path for me; to Dr. Hugh F. Rankin, who graciously gave me permission to make free use of his manuscript study of the eighteenth-century theater in Williamsburg; and to Miss Jane Carson, who not only introduced me to unsuspected source materials but performed the chore of reading the completed manuscript and checking it carefully for errors of omission and commission.

A STAGE FOR ROM

CHAPTER ONE

"Rom. Polly."

The voice was hoarse with pain.

The boy and girl, alike as two coins, answered together, "Hush, Papa."

Polly moved closer to the pile of hay upon which her father lay and wiped his forehead with her kerchief. Rom said, "Don't talk, Papa. The doctor will come soon." He looked at his father's leg, angled back upon itself, the bones showing where they had pierced the skin, and fought the sickness that rose in him.

Barnabas Hormsby lay for a moment, not speaking, gathering in spite of the pain in his leg strength for what he had to do; for what he should have done long ago had he not dreaded to break the strong, sweet bond that held him to Polly and Rom. He wondered how he could soften the tale he must tell them and thought there was no way. The lad and lass must be twelve now—or older—old enough surely to know the truth, such as it was, about themselves. He sighed. Old enough or not they'd have to hear it now. Who could say whether he'd come out of this accident alive.

"No," he said and paused to steady his voice and went on more strongly. "No, Rom. There's no time left for waiting. With such a hurt as this, there's none can see the end and what I have to tell must be told while I've still the strength and the wit to tell it."

Rom's face went, suddenly, white and Polly cried out softly.

"Now, now, bairns," Barnabas Hormsby said and tried to smile encouragement to them. "It'll likely not come to what we're fearing. But we'll take no chance. Come, give me your hands and listen well."

They sat on the rough floor of the barn, one on each side of him, conscious of the rich, warm smell of drying left over from last year's tobacco that still filled the place. Each of them took one of the damp hands and held it tight and prepared to listen.

"It's a story I have to tell you, bairns, a story of a thing that happened ten years gone."

He looked at their sober faces and hated what he had to do.

"A wet day it was in May. The year was 1742. My Susan was getting the supper when I closed the shop and called to her I'd step down to the Red Lion to hear news of the day."

He remembered that day well. The blossoms on the horse chestnut trees shone through the rain like giant candles, pink and white, and bluebells lifted their thirsty cups in all the neat gardens along the crooked streets of Petersfield.

"The inn was uncommon empty. No more than a handful of folk were there, and they all clustering in the middle of the room and chattering. Frank Browning, the innkeeper, stood tall among them and scratched his head.

"'What's afoot then, Frank?' I called as I came through the door. 'Trouble, Barney,' he said, 'or I'm a Dutchman. Trouble and likely the devil to pay to boot. Come and see.'

"The cluster broke up then and I saw."

He had forgotten his leg in remembering and moved it and the pain ran along his whole body and stopped his speaking. He waited a little until the hurt eased somewhat. Rom and Polly tightened their hands on his, but they did not speak.

"What I saw was two mites of humanity—a boy and a girl, as like as two golden sovereigns, sitting upon a large and stout case of fine leather."

"But, Papa," Rom began, not glimpsing yet the end of the story.

"Wait, Rom," Barnabas said. "Hear me to the end. When I'd got my mouth closed again (for it's not a common thing to find two stranger bairns of two years or three alone in the common room of an inn), Frank Browning told me how a young man well, even handsomely, dressed, had brought the twins (for such they surely were) in a traveling chaise and left them—his niece and nephew he called them—and their box in Frank's care. He had, the young man explained, an errand in the neighborhood. It would not take him above an hour and he begged Frank's goodwill in keeping an eye upon the young ones. They would, he promised, give him no trouble, being gently bred. Nor, indeed, had they.

"But the hour passed and another and another. Frank had waited, in all, some five hours by the clock on the shelf and had then sent his potboy to look for the young stranger. The potboy and, in the end, half the town of Petersfield had looked and inquired and found nor hide nor hair nor sign of the man. He had disappeared into the air or walked invisible across the downs. Frank, I can tell you, was wild with worry, for he was a lone man with no wife nor sister and he'd no notion of the needs of children.

3

It was then I had an idea. My Susan and I, we had no children . . ."

Rom and Polly drew sharp breaths, seeing, blindingly now, the meaning in the story. They spoke together (as, being twins, they often did) in quick denial, "No, Papa, no!" but Barnabas Hormsby did not heed their plea to be told this thing was untrue. He went on as if they had not broken their silence, though his heart ached for the misery in their faces.

"We had no children, but we had room in the house over the printing shop, and I knew Susan would welcome the left ones. And so I told Frank and so it was arranged. The potboy was called to bring along the box and I took the two of you home to my Susan."

He waited, then, for a comment from them, but it did not come, for now the two beside him were held still in the shock of discovering the man and woman they had known as father and mother for all the years of their remembering were in truth no kin of theirs. Barnabas went on with his story, trying not to see in the sun that showered golden light in bands through the open door of the tobacco barn, the blank, whipped look upon their faces.

"We thought, my Susan and I, the gentleman who had left you would come again and take you away and that right soon. But he did not. Six weeks later a shepherd's dog found him—or what was left of him—upon the downs. He'd been shot through the head and robbed and hidden in a shallow grave in a lonely place. It was only by his clothes Frank knew him. We tried then—every way we tried—to get news of two children lost, but we got none and, in time, we kept you for our own and cherished you with love and kindness as our own until my Susan died and we three took to wandering the towns and fairs of England and came at last across the sea to America."

He stopped and closed his eyes against his own pain and the pain he had caused the two he loved so well. Beyond the door of the barn a mockingbird filled the still July

4

morning with his stolen songs. Inside the barn there was no sound to break through the emptiness in the minds of the two who had lost their identity and the one who feared he might lose his life.

A new sound, a rush of hoofbeats on the hard-packed dirt, broke into the silence and into the heavy spell upon them. Rom got up, moved stiffly like a man long held in bonds toward the barn door, and Polly followed him. He shaded his eyes against the sun's blare and said, "It's the doctor, likely," and waited.

The doctor pulled his horse out of a gallop and slid from his back and tied him to a sapling beside the barn door. The stunned look on the two faces brought pity for the handsome youngsters and he spoke to cheer them.

"Do you not look as if the world is ending, young sir and young mistress. I am Dr. Peter Hay and no doubt I can make do to fix a simple broken leg fast enough."

Rom forced his mind from the story they'd just heard. The doctor's face was kind and, at another time, he would have taken courage from it. Now there were too many new thoughts beating at him, muddying his thinking and confusing what had been, so short a time ago, his only concern. He tried to speak to this Dr. Hay and could not. It was Polly, always the more practical, who said, "We hope so, sir. But it is none so simple, this broken leg. Will you come in, sir, and see it for yourself. Our—father, Barnabas Hormsby, is within the barn and in great pain."

They followed Dr. Hay in through the door. They heard him rumble something to himself as he knelt beside Barnabas to explore the damaged leg, but they could not tell the words.

Barnabas said, with an effort, "Good of you to come all this way so quickly for a stranger, sir," and Dr. Hay growled again, hushing him, and looked at Rom and Polly and shook his head a very little. "I'm afraid I must hurt you, sir," he said, "perhaps it were best . . ."

He did not need to finish the sentence. Barnabas said,

5

"Rom, you and Polly go and see to Betsy and the caravan. The mare's not had her oats this day, and the caravan likely needs tidying."

They said together, "No, Papa," the familiar, loved name coming without thought, and he interrupted them sternly, in the voice that had always meant an order to be obeyed without question. "Do as I say, Romulus and Polly." Polly leaned down to kiss him and took Rom's hand and together they went out into the brilliant day and around the tangle of rope that had caused the accident, and the leather box with puppets half in and half out of it, to the meadow where the farmer had given them permission to leave their caravan in return for entertainment for himself and his wife and their multiplication of tumbling children.

They did not speak until they came to the gay wagon that had been their home for three years. They had lumbered in it along the roads of England, taking their traveling show from fair to fair and from market town to market town until Barnabas had told them one day, after he had been to London Town on some mystery of his own, that they were going to the Colonies. The caravan had looked forlorn when they had dismantled it piece by piece and wrapped the pieces in heavy cloth and piled them upon the cart that would take them to London, to the sloop *Morning Star* bound for Yorktown in the Colony of Virginia. But when the long voyage was done and they had put the pieces into their own proper places again and the wagon stood whole once more, they had felt as if they had come home instead of to a far place.

Today the wagon had no power to welcome them and bring them comfort. Its gaiety seemed only to mock their double despair.

Polly leaned her head on the yellow door swung back against the blue side, and Rom kicked the red wheel. "Who are we, Polly? What are we?" he cried out and the words were filled with a sense of emptiness where once

6

there had been the warm knowledge of family. Even the caravan seemed no more than a symbol of impermanence, a reminder that they were wanderers in a foreign land, without even a fixed place to live.

Polly straightened away from the door and came to stand beside him, her shoulder touching his for comfort. "Well," she said slowly, thinking about each word before she spoke it, "I suppose we're still—ourselves, really—still Rom and Polly. Just as we've always been. Nothing can change that."

He made an impatient gesture. "Oh, *that*. Of course we're ourselves. But what does that mean? Everybody's *himself*. I mean, where do we *belong*? Who do we belong *to*? Those are the important questions." His sense of their loss, of being alone with nobody to belong to, made his voice rough and angry.

Polly lifted her shoulders in the gesture she used when he was being difficult. She, too, had been shocked at first by Barney's story. But now she'd had a little time to think about it she couldn't see it made much difference. She was Polly and he was Romulus and Barnabas Hormsby was still the man who had been the best kind of father to them, and she didn't see that anything else mattered. "I don't see that anything's changed, Rom," she said, "anything important. Why do you fret so?"

"Because," he said, "because—don't you *see*, Polly—we don't even have a name!"

"Who cares? Hormsby's a good name—as good as any other. It's not your name that counts. It's you." She wanted to understand why he was so disturbed, especially because this was the first time she could remember they had not thought alike on something really important. But she couldn't see why he kept nagging at it. And she felt herself getting more and more irritated by what seemed his stubbornness.

He looked at her sullenly. Couldn't she understand anything? "Don't you see what this means, Pol? We—are—

7

not—anybody. We—have—no—name, no—place. How can we hold up our heads ever again? How can we walk proudly, not knowing who we are? We've—we've nobody and no place to belong to. We *are* nobody."

He could tell by the look on her face she didn't care. He could tell none of it mattered to her, that she thought him silly and stubborn. Almost he hated her.

She said again, reasonably, "Don't fret so, Rom. It's not the end of the world. Besides, you can't do anything about it. No doubt when Papa's better he'll tell us . . ."

"He's *not* our papa. Don't keep calling him that!" He interrupted her with violence, and her anger flared to meet it. She stamped her foot and shouted at him, "Well, he's *my* papa, I'll have you know, Romulus Hormsby. He's always been—been wonderful to us and now he's—he's likely going to d-d-die. And all you can think of is your silly old *pride*. What good is pride, anyway?"

He looked at her, his face crumbling between anger and hurt and a kind of shamed certainty that she was, in a way, right. Anger won and he spoke out of it. "If that's the way you feel, Polly No-name, there's nothing more to talk about." He turned from her and walked away toward the end of the meadow where the small mare they had bought yesterday in Yorktown cropped the sweet grass contentedly.

She let him go. She even laughed a little to herself because he did look ridiculous stalking away, holding his shoulders stiff and straight in dignity here in a meadow empty of any life except herself and the horse and one bright blue bird that soared singing above them. The laughter didn't last. She felt, suddenly, a great pity for her brother whose feelings were so easily torn. She started to go after him and checked herself and sat down on the steps of the caravan, thinking the mare would bring him more of comfort now than she could.

What was happening in the tobacco barn, she wondered. She knew little about such things, but she remem-

8

bered the man in England who had fallen and broken his leg so the bones showed through and had later died, they said, from a poison in his blood. Would their father— all right, their foster-father but none the less dear for that —die too? She could not suffer the thought and she turned her mind away from it to the morning that seemed a good year long though the sun had not yet passed the noon point.

It was, she realized with a sense of shock, a Sunday. It had begun with joy, for they had promised Harry Struthers, the kind farmer, to give their show for him and his family that day and they liked to give their show. While Papa and Rom busied themselves with breakfast, she had spread their beds quickly—hers in the curtained cubicle at the end of the caravan, Papa's and Rom's in the cunningly built bunks along the caravan's sides that served them all as seats in the daytime. They had eaten quickly and gone to the house yard. She and Rom had set up the folding stage they had made for the puppets, while Papa tested the doorposts of the stable and found them tight and well-set in the ground and fastened the rope firmly for his ropedancing.

Firmly but not firmly enough, she thought. How else explain what had happened? She and Rom and the puppets they called the Little People had delighted the whole Struthers family with the madcap doings of Harlequin. Then Papa, in his best spangly costume that glittered brave as gold in the Virginia sun, climbed to the little platform that held the balls and pipes, the chairs and wands he would balance on his nose and fingers while he walked and danced upon the slack rope. They knew by heart how it would be for they had seen it each day since they could remember as he took time from his work to practice his father's art and his grandfather's behind the small house in Petersfield. They had, in fact, seen it so often they had grown out of wonder at the skill and precision that enabled him to go through the positions of

9

standing and kneeling and sitting and running upon the thin hemp strands while he added wand to wand and balanced them on his fingers. She and Rom had turned away and begun to store the puppet theater and the Little People safe within their leather box.

They had not seen the accident, had had no warning of disaster, until they heard Mrs. Struthers scream and turned to find Barnabas Hormsby, the most skillful rope-dancer of them all, lying white and still upon the ground in his spangles, his leg torn and doubled backward beneath him.

The farmer and his eldest son had, when the first shock was over, sprung to Barney's side and lifted him gently. They had thought to take him to the caravan, to his own bed, but the pain that came with movement had been too great and he had cried out fiercely, and they had laid him upon a pile of hay, fresh cut, on the floor of the tobacco barn. Harry Struthers had sent another of his boys to Williamsburg to fetch the doctor, while the twins sat beside their father.

Sat beside him and discovered he was not their father. She tried to feel as Rom felt, that this knowledge held some deep affront to their pride, to their very being—that it was somehow shameful not to know their true name. But she could not. Rom was so often difficult, so ready to find an affront where none was and to hold it close.

She sighed. What was Rom thinking now? She half moved with the thought she'd best go to him after all and try to bring him comfort. But she did not finish the movement. His griefs were always better shared with the dumb creatures or with his Little People. Even the earth itself, she thought, had more power to ease his sorrow than any human being. She'd best let him be.

CHAPTER TWO

Rom dug his head into Betsy's side. The mare whinnied softly as if she understood and would help him if she could. The July sun beat upon him. He could feel the sweat running under the neckband of his plain stock and plastering the white cotton shirt to his back, but he was, for the first time since they had known the searing heat of a Virginia summer, unmindful of it.

He wondered whether anybody else in all the world's long ages had felt so forlorn, had so suddenly lost his identity and become as a stranger even to himself. He thought there could be nothing worse than to stop knowing who you are—to become a nobody. One minute he had been Romulus Hormsby, son of Barnabas Hormsby, printer and ropedancer, and his wife Susan, dead these three years. One minute he had had remembered roots, a birthright in his own town of Petersfield. One minute he had been part of a whole, secure world. And then . . . Between one long breath and the next he had become— nothing. A person without a family, without roots in space, without even a name.

"Who am I, Betsy?" He spoke to the horse in a little,

wracked whisper. "What am I? Who is my father? What is he? He—he might be a thief. Or a murderer. Where is he?"

A new question came into his mind, to add its torture to the rest. "Why did he abandon us? Why did he not turn the whole world upside down to find his lost children? Didn't he *want* us?"

A long sob shook his body, and the mare shifted her feet and switched her tail at a great, green fly on her withers. Rom beat upon her shoulder with his fists and she stood patiently until he was quiet. His mind, roaming the empty spaces of unhappiness, found a new resting place. What would become of them if Pa—he remembered he no longer had a father—if *Barney* died of a poison in his blood as the man at Bartholomew Fair had died when he fell and tore his leg? What would they do, he and Polly, alone in a strange and alien land?

She would expect him to know. He was—was almost a man grown and she only a girl. She would look to him to keep her safe and housed and fed. And he—he was afraid.

"Oh, Betsy," he said. "I won't know what to do. I'm so frightened."

Betsy shook her head and he thought she needn't try to deny it. He was a coward and that was sure. He thought of the many times he had run away rather than fight with the other boys, and he wondered how soon Polly and—and Barney would have discovered his weak fears had not Barney decided after Susan's dying to sell his printing shop and go back to the ropedancing he'd learned from his father and loved in his youth. There had been no time for brawling in their wandering life on the English roads and no inclination, for everyone had loved Barney and, for his sake, his youngsters, who were always ready and eager to make their puppet people perform for the pleasure of other strolling entertainers when they rested briefly between the market towns and fairs.

The horse whinnied again. Rom took his head out of her side and put his arms around her neck and wished he had never been born.

Why wouldn't Polly understand? If she had felt as forlorn and forsaken, as—as unidentified as he, his own loneliness would have been less. Polly. She had always understood before. She'd always felt what he felt. But now—now she had become a person apart, no longer as like him in mind as she was in face. He wondered what she was thinking now? Maybe he should not have left her in anger. Maybe he was at fault there too. She was his sister. He should not have acted so to her, no matter how angry he had felt. Maybe she was lonely too, and afraid. But she hadn't seemed afraid. Only—only *stupid*.

She was his sister. His twin. She was, as he was, placeless and nameless in a world that seemed suddenly enormous and empty and without kindness. Yet she didn't seem to care one small bit. He felt as if he had been dragged from a loved and friendly room and plunged, shivering, into an icy stream.

"Rom! R—o—m!"

The call came across the meadow, urgently upon the hot summer wind. He lifted his head and saw Polly beckoning and felt his heart lift because his sister was still his sister and calling him. He gave Betsy's neck a squeeze and turned and ran toward Polly.

"The doctor's waiting for us, and—and I—I'm so frightened for Papa," she said. He put his arm around her and whispered miserably, "I was unkind to be angry, Polly. I ask your forgiveness. I—I . . ."

"Hush, Rom." She smiled a little and laid her finger gently upon his lips. "It doesn't matter. Somehow we will work all this out—together. Now, come, let us go to the doctor."

"Yes," he said, and for the moment forgot he was a nameless nobody, forgot he was alone in an empty world, forgot his fear, remembering only the loved man who had been his father in all things but blood.

Dr. Hay waited for them outside the tobacco barn. They could see he was troubled though he smiled encouragement as they came up to him.

"Papa?" Rom said.

"He's resting now. I've given him some medicine to ease the pain and he should sleep awhile. Come over here, Rom and Polly, to the shade." He led them to a rough bench that circled a great oak tree at the edge of the barnyard and sat down between them. But he did not speak at once and the silence dropped heavy between them as a stone drops into deep, still water.

"Sir?" Rom asked, when he could bear the quiet no longer.

Dr. Hay seemed to shake himself together, though he made no outward movement. "I don't know, Rom," he said. "I've done what I could. But no man can say the end. Had the leg bones, in breaking, not pierced the flesh there would be little danger. The bones would knit themselves together and save for, perhaps, a small limp your father would be as good as new in a little time. But now —I wish I could tell you there would be no trouble. I cannot. I've set the bones and washed the wound. It may be there's no poison in it. If we only *knew* more of these things. Some day—some day we *will* know more."

He seemed to forget them. He seemed to be searching ahead in time, trying to see what the years might bring to the knowledge of healing.

Polly broke his reverie. "Will you tell us, sir, just what the danger is and what we can do to help?"

"We should know by tomorrow, Mistress Polly, whether there is poison in the wound. If this be so your father will be flushed and hot with fever. He will be restless even when he sleeps and he may speak wildly, as a man bereft of his senses, but he will not be mad. There is little you can do and more's the pity, for it's ever easier to watch the suffering of one you love if there is somewhat of help to be given. Keep cooling cloths upon his head. Keep him as quiet as you can. Give him the medicinal herbs I shall leave with you as I direct you to give them. Stay by him. Try not to fear. I will come each day to bleed him and

14

watch him. Do you not lose heart. Should the poison and its fever rage in his body yet I have hope for him. He is strong of heart and wind. It is clear he has not abused his body and it is tough and ready for a fight."

He looked at them and they, together, nodded understanding of what he had told them, but they could not speak of it. Rom saw Polly close her eyes and saw her fingers, laced in her lap, tighten and bite once into the backs of her hands. Then she opened her eyes and relaxed her hands and he knew she was thinking, no use to borrow trouble. Let us wait to see what tomorrow brings and save our strength for what may come, and he knew she was right and tried to free his mind, too, of fear.

"One thing more," Dr. Hay said. "I should like to take your father to town, to lodge him in my own house. But I fear to move him now more than is necessary. Struthers would gladly bed him but he has no bed to spare, nor yet enough for his own family. Your father told me, before I sent him off to sleep, that you have brought a snug caravan from England and are living in it now. Do you, Mistress Polly and Rom, think you can make do to care for him there?"

"Yes," they said together. "It will be better so," Rom added. "He loves the caravan and has been happier there than elsewhere since our—" he stumbled but went on firmly, not wanting to make explanations to the doctor now, "since our mother died."

"It is good," Dr. Hay said. "It may well be he will mend the faster in such a place. Struthers and his sons will help you move him when he has rested a little longer. And I will come again tomorrow."

He looked at the two unhappy, worried faces and added gently. "Lift up your hearts. Do not let fear banish hope. Good-by until tomorrow and—and God bless and keep you both."

He went from them toward the sapling where his horse stood patiently waiting. After a moment Rom, forcing his mind from its daze of worry and pain, ran after him. "We cannot thank you properly, sir," he said, "for your kindness to us who are strangers newly come to your country. I . . ."

Dr. Hay interrupted him. "No, no lad, it's nothing. We are, many of us, newcomers here and all of us, even those who have put down their roots in Virginia and have learned to love her as you will, are well and kindly disposed to the folk who still come." He looked closely at Rom and seemed to see some of his fear for the clouded future. "Do not be afraid, Rom Hormsby. Whatever comes you

will find friends here and good people to help you should you need help."

Rom felt some of the heaviness lift from his heart. He said, "Thank you again, Dr. Hay," and added haltingly for the embarrassment he felt, "I don't know, sir, what moneys my—we have. But we—Polly and I—we shall somehow find your fee."

"Bless you, Rom," Dr. Hay said gruffly, for he found himself reaching out to this boy who seemed bent with some heavy grief, "do you not burden your mind with worry over fees. While I was waiting for you but now I was examining your puppets. They are rarely made and like none I have seen before. They are, I think, very old and likely of Italian workmanship. If, when your father is well again, you will make them play for me and my friends some evening, I shall consider myself well paid for whatever service I can do for you and Mistress Polly."

"Oh, sir, you are kind," Rom said, but he doubted he'd been heard for Dr. Hay had mounted into his saddle with one deft, quick movement and was already urging his roan gelding along the farm lane.

Polly pushed the hair back from her forehead. It was dank and heavy with sweat. It needed washing but there had been no time between the hours of tending the fever-ridden man upon the bed and the minutes—or so it seemed —of snatched sleep. She went to the door of the caravan seeking a little coolness in the still heat. The air, moisture-filled, gave her no relief. It was as if she breathed lint long soaked in water. How long had it been since Papa's accident? How long since the fever had fought his will for possession of his body? She tried to count the days and could not. Each gray hour ran into the next, with nothing to distinguish one from the other or show them separate and distinct.

Each day Dr. Hay had come and cleaned the festering wound and done what else was needful and smiled at them and gone away. Each day she and Rom had sat beside the laboring, wasting form upon the bed, changing headcloths, forcing a little barley water down the dry throat, giving the medicines the doctor ordered, taking turn and turn about to watch and sleep and watch again, forcing themselves to eat the food Mrs. Struthers sent them.

("Do you not worry, young ones," Mrs. Struthers had said when Rom protested at the time and cost she was pouring out for them, "it's been a good year for the crops. We've enough and more than enough to spare. Better eaten than wasted. And when I'm cooking for twelve already, what's another mouth or two to me?")

Polly's eyes were weighted with tiredness and watching. It would soon be time for Dr. Hay to come. Then she would call Rom and they would help the doctor as they could, and then she would get into the cubicle and fall into the mussed sheets on the bed, already hot from Rom's sleeping, and forget trouble for a few hours.

The caravan was very still. Too still. For the first time in many days there was no sound of heavy breathing, no half-voiced cries or moans or restless turning. She whirled from the door and ran to the bed, fear stopping her breath.

Papa was dead! She was sure of it. She had left him and he had come to the end of his struggle and let the fever win and she had not been beside him. She looked at Barney and saw his eyes closed and his body as still as death itself. She knelt beside the bed and put her hand out to touch the waxlike skin of his face.

At first she did not know the meaning of what she felt. She did not believe it was Barney's face, so moist and cool. It must be her own fingers she was feeling. This was what Dr. Hay had told them to watch for, the first sign that the fever was gone, the battle won. She stared stupidly at Barney until he opened his eyes and said, in a voice so weak and low she hardly heard it, "Polly?"

18

"Oh, Papa," she said, and thought she could not move for relief. "Oh, Papa."

He tried to raise his hand but he had not the strength. His eyes smiled at her and he said slowly, "All—right—now. Rom?"

"I'll get him, Papa. Do you rest."

She moved aside the curtain and put her hand softly on Rom's shoulder. He came awake at once and started up and saw her face wet with tears. "He is dead!" he said in a flat voice and she caught his hand, shaking her head, giving him no time to wash the sleep from his eyes, pulling him through the curtain. "No," she said, "no, no, no. The fever's *gone*. He's going to get well."

Rom thought his legs would not hold him upright. They felt boneless, unmuscled with the relief that shook him. He leaned for a moment against the side of the caravan, waiting for strength to come back to him. She tugged at him impatiently and he freed his hand and caught her in a great hug and she felt his body shaken and knew he was sobbing inside himself.

"Come," she said, whispering. "He wants you," and they went together to the bed and saw that Barnabas Hormsby had not stayed for their coming but was sleeping quietly and naturally.

They stood watching him, knowing a pleasure they had not known before in his quiet breathing. They did not know Dr. Hay had come until each felt a strong arm guiding them away toward the door of the caravan and heard, "Thank you, Lord, for your infinite goodness and mercy," spoken so gently the words scarcely troubled the heavy air.

They sat upon the caravan steps and none of them cared now that the day was breathless, the clouds piled on the horizon heavy with thunder. "He *will* get well now, Dr. Hay?" Polly asked, suddenly afraid to believe the long fight was done.

"He will, Mistress Polly, thanks to the good Lord and

his own strong body and will and the nursing you and Rom have given him. He will sleep, I think, until tomorrow and will likely have a mighty hunger on him when he wakes. Give him simple food at first, in small amounts and often. And do you and Rom sleep yourselves, for he will still need care and, unless he's different from most, he'll fret and be troublesome before he can be up and about again. I'll come again tomorrow. But do you sleep. We want no more invalids in this caravan. Sleep's the best doctor. So get you to bed."

Rom said, "Yes," in a voice that showed for the first time the weariness he had tried to keep hidden. Polly laughed and ran her fingers through her hair. "Not I," she said, "not until I've washed my hair and had a proper bath in the creek."

CHAPTER THREE

"How do you feel, Papa?" Polly asked.

A week had gone since Barnabas Hormsby's fever broke, and each day he had grown stronger and, as Dr. Hay had predicted, more fretful because he could not be up and about his business. He lay, quietly now, and watched Polly busy about the caravan, tidying it for the day, while Rom prepared their breakfast outside.

"Well enough, lass," he growled to her question. "Too well to be lying idle abed for the sake of a mending leg. When will that villain, Dr. Hay, let me up? Or has he told you?"

"Don't fret, Papa," she urged him. "Bones don't mend quickly, and Dr. Hay will not keep you abed a day longer than need be. Here's Rom. We'll prop you up for breakfast."

They took his shoulders and helped him raise himself in

the bed and put behind him a rough rack of boards Rom had made to support him. He's still weak as a day-old kitten, Polly thought, and no wonder, but he's gaining every day.

Rom went back to his cooking fire, while Polly got out cups and plates from a cupboard cunningly concealed under Rom's bunk. When Rom had brought in a jug of steaming tea, a pone of cornbread baked, as Mrs. Struthers had taught him, in the ashes, and strips of thick, fragrant bacon, they ate their breakfast in silence, each of them intent upon his own thoughts.

Polly watched Rom. He had been overquiet, brooding, for the past three days, keeping away from her and from Barney whenever he could, though he never shirked his share of caring for the convalescent. He was brooding now, dark head bent over his plate, and Polly thought, he's back to fretting because we've no proper parents. As if it mattered.

He had been, during the time Barney fought the fever for his life, too concerned or too tired to think about himself or his own problems. But now that all was well again he'd drawn apart from them and nursed his particular grief. Polly had tried to talk to him about it, tried to make him see it didn't matter so long as they were all alive and together, tried to cheer him or, at least, tease him out of his gloom. It had done no good. He had heard her patiently when she spoke and when she had done, walked quietly from her. She had guessed he was waiting until Barney was strong enough to answer questions. She feared, watching the tension in his body as he ate his breakfast, that he was about to put his questions now and she wondered how she could stop him. She wanted Papa to have more strength before he was troubled.

Rom set his plate on the floor and got up from the stool. He stood for a moment looking down at Barney before he said, "Sir. Sir, I would ask . . ."

Polly interrupted him quickly, "Come, Rom, help me

22

clear away the dishes," but he did not even look at her.

"Sir," he began again, "I would . . ."

Polly pulled at the sleeve of his shirt. "No, Rom," she whispered, "not yet."

Barney said quietly but with the first authority he'd shown since his fall, "Be quiet, lass, and let him speak. I know what he would say and I'm ready for it. To say true, I will be glad to finish what I started in the tobacco barn yonder."

He reached out and took Rom's hand and looked at him with understanding. "I was not kind to you, lad," he said, "to you or to Polly, though I doubt the hurt cuts so deep with her. It was not a kind thing to spring upon you with my tale. If I'd brought you quiet-like to the gate you'd have taken it like any good horse. You know, lad, it's none so easy to break a habit of thinking once it's set and I reckoned I'd plenty of time, until I found myself there upon my back and death standing looking at me from the shadows of that barn."

"But, sir," Rom began stubbornly, not one bit eased by Barney's words, and Barney said, "Come, lad. You'd best call me Barney, since I can well see you've no mind to name me father when I'm not."

Rom said, "I'm—I'm sorry, sir—Barney—that it is so."

"You've no cause to be sorry, Rom. You mind how Old Will Shakespeare said, 'What's in a name? A rose by any other name' and so forth." He grinned at Rom, teasing him.

Rom shifted his feet uncertainly. He had not expected Barney to see so far into his mind and understand what he saw and make light of it.

"Well, now," Barney said, "ask your questions, lad. I'm ready for you."

Rom shuffled again. Now that the time had come and Barney so ready to talk, his questions seemed, suddenly, vanished. He moved his shoulders and fumbled with the fastening of his belt. Barney waited, watching him, wondering how best to help him.

"Bring me my traveling case," he said when it was clear Rom's tongue was not coming untied. Rom went to the end of the caravan and came back with a stout box covered in rough green cloth and put it on the bed beside Barney. Polly brought forward the two stools and she and Rom sat and waited while Barney felt about the box lid until he found a hidden spring and released it. The lid snapped open but he did not throw it wide at once.

Rather, he began slowly and carefully, as if he tested each word to see if it would bear its full weight of meaning, to talk. "You mind I told you of the stout, leather box left with you at the inn by the man who named himself your uncle?"

They nodded.

"What that box held was all we could look to, to find out who you were. Except for the clothes—good clothes of fine cloth and workmanship—which you two wore out entirely, everything in it has been close-kept these ten years."

"What—what *was* in it?" Polly asked, and Rom hitched his stool a bit closer to the bed.

"First," Barney looked at Rom, "your Little People and their gear."

Rom drew in his breath before he said, "The Little People came with us! I had thought they were your grandfather's, like the balls and wands." This knowledge lifted his heart a little. There was a kind of belonging for him if his beloved puppets had always been theirs.

"No," Barney was saying. "My father and his father before him were jugglers and ropedancers, not carvers of wood or makers of theater. The Little People are your birthright, Rom. Yours and Polly's. We hoped at first they might lead us to your true parents, but they did not."

Rom nodded, but his eyes were a little less bleak than they had been. Polly said, "What else was in the box?"

"A stack of golden sovereigns. These I used for you as I will tell you later. And—two bits of paper."

He opened the lid of the box and brought out two pieces of paper. One of them, discolored with age and torn on the edges, was printed on one side. The other, written by hand, had, it was plain, at one time been crumpled into a ball and later smoothed out again. Barney spread the first upon the coverlet so that the two beside him could read the words upon it.

Rom and Polly studied it. They had not seen anything like it before and their faces showed puzzlement.

"What is it, Papa?" Polly asked. "Some of it is so smudged. I can't make it out and the rest . . ." She let her lifted shoulders finish the sentence for her.

Barney shook himself. "My head must still be weak," he said. "I had forgotten you'd neither of you seen a ticket to a playhouse, for all that Rom spends every spare hour reading Old Will Shakespeare's plays that belonged to my father." His eye went to a small shelf of books in the corner. "I'll warrant you have the lot of them by heart. Now what was I saying?"

"About this, Papa." Polly touched the paper.

"Yes. Well, now, this is a ticket for an actor's benefit. And here's the why of it. Every leading actor in a company of players is allowed, each season, one benefit performance. And that, mind you, is in addition to his regular share of the company's profits, if indeed there be any. The actor gets, at his benefit, the lion's share of all moneys taken in, but he, himself, must sell the tickets for his own show. Now this bit of paper is such a benefit ticket. For an actor named Patrick Malone. He was evidently touring the provinces with a company of comedians and was allowed his benefit at Bath in the year 1742. He must have been a good actor and able to sing a bit because he played, at his benefit, the leading role in Mr. Gay's *Beggar's Opera.*"

Rom said, "That would be the part of Macheath," and Barney nodded. "But B—Barney, what has all this to do with us?" Rom went on.

"The ticket, Rom, the ticket. What do you use for wits,

boy?" Barney roared at him, his irritation rising. The next minute he apologized, seeing the surprise in Rom's eyes. "I'm sorry, Rom. If I could just get out of this—this—this devil-sent bunk and get around again I'd not be so touchy. Well, now lad, this is what it means to you and Polly. This ticket was caught in the very bottom of the box when my Susan and I went through it seeking a sign of who you were. We talked about it, she and I, a time and a time again and we figured it this way. Nobody in his right mind would pay seven shillings and sixpence for a box seat—for such this is—and then stay away from the play. If he were prevented from going himself by some unexpected thing, he'd surely give his ticket to a friend. And the person who used the ticket would have to give it up at the door. Else he'd not be let in by the doorkeeper. Right?"

Rom and Polly nodded. They could find no fault with this reasoning.

"So—we figured it out, my Susan and I, *this* ticket was one Patrick Malone could not sell. He tossed it into his box and went on his way and forgot it."

"Then," Rom said slowly, "then you think this—this Patrick Malone was—is—our real father?"

"That I do, Rom."

"But," Polly objected, "what about the Little People? If this Malone was a—a live actor why would he carry puppets with him?"

"We considered that too, Polly. The Little People may have been left over from another kind of life and he could not bear to part with them. They are very old, you know, and no doubt valuable. They may have been a legacy from his father or his grandfather, like my wands and balls. Or he may have been keeping them for a friend. Or he may have had them as another string to his bow—so when times were bad for actors he could wander the towns and fairs as we did. I mind my father telling me when he prenticed me to a printer to improve my place in life, 'Keep the wands and balls, Barney, and keep the skill to use them.

Then, when times are bad and printing won't make you a living, you can yet go about and about ropedancing for there'll always be some will have coins to throw at such as we.' "

Rom was frowning, and Barney said, "What is it, Rom? What troubles you?"

"A score of things," Rom said. "To begin with, what good is it—this guessing at a name for our father? Do you know where he is? Can we find him? Why did he leave us? Whence came those fine clothes? And why was the box with the Little People left at the inn with us? Who was . . ."

"Softly, lad," Barney said, laughing. "One thing at a time. You mind the day I left you and went up to London Town in the winter of the year?"

They nodded.

"I went there to try to find the answers to some of those very questions. I've a friend there who's always hankered after the acting trade though he'd no aptness for it. He was a wigmaker and lived near Covent Garden so he could be among the people he liked the best and admired the most. I was sure he'd know a bit about Patrick Malone if anyone would and I thought the time had come to do more than wander about with my ears open. (Yes, that was my reason for selling the shop and taking the road with you when my Susan died.) So, I asked my friend for word of Patrick Malone since I could get none myself. He knew the name well enough but not the whereabouts of the man. But my friend had friends and he soon got news of this Malone. News, at least, of a sort. It was said Malone had joined a traveling company and gone off to the Colonies, for he had an itching foot. No one knew what company he had joined or where in the Colonies they were bound. It was no more than rumor but it was the first thing I'd found and I went straightway to the dockside and used those golden sovereigns I'd been keeping for you to buy our passages on the first ship outward bound for America. It seemed to me I could make no better use of them than to find your father—or try to—and I knew that once we were across the water we could make our way well enough throughout the Colonies."

Rom said, "Yes. I suppose we can," and wished with all his heart he need never take the road again but could settle here—or somewhere—in some permanent home. "But it doesn't seem a very large hope, does it?" he added.

Barney's face, which had been eager and smiling, crumpled in disappointment, and Polly said quickly, "Do you not be so easily disheartened, Rom. Who can say? This Patrick Malone may as well come to Williamsburg for all you know. At least we've made a beginning, since you're so bound and determined to find our father. For myself, I'm happy as I am but I think it was clever of Papa to find out so much. What about the other paper, Papa?"

Barney looked at her gratefully, but he still sounded unsure of himself when he answered, "It's not so clear in its meaning. Still, it was a writing and it was in the box along with the other things. It had been wadded tight and used as a kind of support for the King Puppet's head along with other paper that was blank. It looked as if whoever had packed up the box had lacked a bit for the King and took whatever was nearest to hand, not paying too much mind to what it was. So—we kept it." He handed her the mussed paper. "Do you read it out, Polly."

She smoothed the paper carefully. It was, she thought, but a part of a letter. The top had been torn from the sheet. The writing was beautiful—graceful and clear and flowing—each letter carefully lined out in what must have been very black ink, which had turned brown with time. A single initial—it might have been a P or an R—and a date, 20 April 1742, stood together at the bottom of the page, scribbled as if the writer, coming to the end in haste, had taken less pains with his writing. She read the rest of the words slowly, aloud: "'. . . know how you feel on these matters. Your heart was ever stronger to rule your actions

28

than your head. Despite your love and care you must be rid of them—both of them—and that right quickly. In these hard times there is no place for weak sentiment. What you must do, do quickly, and come straightly to us. The King has need of you.'"

She finished reading and heard a strangled sound from Rom and looked up and found him on his feet, his hands made into fists, his face red as the caravan's wheels.

"Rom," she cried, "what is it?" and Barney stretched out a hand to him and said, "Rom, Rom. What is distressing you? Are you ill, lad? Has the long strain of nursing me . . ."

Rom had been choking on his own emotion. Now he managed to clear his voice, which came out in a great angry shout. "Oh, you are blind, you two. Blind and deaf. Did you not *hear* what that—that letter said? How can you sit so, your mouths agape at me as if I were suddenly gone mad? You *heard* it."

Polly looked at the letter again, wondering what she had read that so distressed him. Barney said sternly, "Mind your manners, Romulus. And if you have anything to say, say it quietly and politely. There's nothing in that letter to cause such raging. I've read it many a time and I know. Sit down and behave yourself."

The stern, cold voice steadied Rom a little. He went to the end of the caravan and dipped a gourd into a wooden bucket of water and drank thirstily and came back and sat down while the others waited and watched. He could feel the heated blood drawing away from his face and he made himself think of the bright August sky and the green meadow and Betsy under the tulip tree at its end until he could be sure of speaking calmly. Then he reached over and took the letter from Polly's hand and coughed and read: " 'Despite your love and care you must be rid of them—both of them—and that right quickly.' "

He looked at them and saw their faces still blank and

29

calm and wanted to shout at them again and forced himself to quiet.

"Well?" Polly said. There was nothing here, she thought, to rouse him so.

Rom said, "Don't you *see? 'You must be rid of them—both of them—and that right quickly.'* Who are *they?* Us, of course, Polly and Rom. Somebody is told we must be got rid of quickly. In spite of someone's love and care. We must . . ."

"Romulus!"

Barney stopped him, and then went on quietly. "This is nonsense. You are reading into those words what is most likely not there. You do not even know they were written to anyone who had you in charge. Besides, *them* may be a pair of cooing doves for all you know. Use your wits, boy."

"Barney!" Rom said, still fighting not to shout. "Do you, begging your pardon, use *your* wits. Is not this letter signed with a P?"

"Or it might be an R," Polly said, and Barney nodded.

"Signed with a P," Rom went on as if they had agreed with him. "The date at the end shows it was written on the twentieth of April, 1742. We were abandoned by our precious uncle or whoever he was in May."

He looked at Barney, and Barney nodded.

"It's plain as your own broken leg," Rom went on. "This fine father of ours, this Patrick Malone, wanted none of his children. Ordered us got rid of, he did. And you, Barnabas Hormsby, have dragged us to this—this heaven-forsaken place at the end of nowhere to find him. To find a man who wanted us lost and cared not how it was done. Well, you find him if you wish and if you can. You and Polly. But leave me out of it."

He threw the letter back on the coverlet and went to the door and turned back to them and said, "I don't want to find him. I don't want to see him. Ever."

He cleared the three steps of the caravan in a single jump and began to run toward the end of the meadow.

Polly started after him, but Barney reached out and caught her skirt and held her. "Let him go, lass," he said quietly. "He was ever one to make a play of simple things. He'll think better of it after a while and see it's only his own imagining put such a light upon innocent words. He's overwrought still from finding himself nameless but you'll see. Leave him be now. He'll come to his own good senses in his own good time."

CHAPTER FOUR

Rom did not, as Barney had predicted, come to his senses. The more he thought on the letter, the surer he was he knew the meaning of those hard words. They were scratched on his brain. They went with him everywhere, even in his sleep. Barney and Polly argued with him, hammered at him as the days shortened toward the autumn and Barney grew stronger and began to hobble about upon the crutch Rom had made for him. Every time he was near them they were at him again, declaring him wrong, saying he had no cause nor right to believe the words meant what he knew they did mean. In the end he took to leaving the caravan at sunup with a bit of food in his pocket and roaming the woods and fields or sitting beside the stream with one of Old Will Shakespeare's plays until the night came down and he could go home and sneak into his bunk in peace.

He wished, darkly, he could leave them and run to some far place and, in time, make his way back to England where he could once more feel secure in surroundings that he knew. But he could not, in fairness, take the Little People with him since they belonged to Polly too and he could not bear to go without them. Barney had said they were his birthright and, no matter how abandoned he and Polly had been, the Little People had still the power to bring him some sort of comfort. So he stayed and avoided Polly and Barney by day and gradually the first blinding hurt of the letter had faded a little and he could see the still, lazy beauty of this new country and feel its peace.

On a day in late August, Polly came seeking him and found him by the stream. She sat down beside him and pulled off her shoes and her white thread stockings and swung her feet into the cool, clear water and said no word. She could feel antagonism in his silence and see it in the stiff way he held his book, pretending to read though his eyes did not move. But she sat on and waited, hoping he would relax if she did not talk.

A quarter of an hour passed and she thought she could not keep silent much longer. She would have to go away and wait and try again to break through his withdrawal. She had to break through it somehow. She had to talk to him, tell him the truth the doctor had told them, persuade him to talk with her and with Papa long enough at least to plan something for their future. But perhaps this was not the time.

She took one foot from the stream, readying herself to leave, and felt his hand upon hers on the grass bank of the stream and eased her foot back into the water and looked at him. His eyes were misty as if he wanted to cry but would not and his voice was rough. "Polly, it is a fair land

and not—not heaven-forsaken. I—I like it, Polly. I—I think I could live my life out here if—if it were my right."

"Do you not cry now, you simpleton," she told herself fiercely, and said aloud to him, "Yes. It is fair. And the people—those we've seen—are fair and kind."

"I—I've not behaved very well, these days past, running from you and—and Barney. That is over now, I think. If—if you and he will only leave off about the letter. I—I know I'm right. I know it. And you will not change my thinking. So it's no good, anyway, to keep at me about it."

She could feel rising tension in the hand that still lay upon hers and she said, quickly, "We know, Rom. We both know we were wrong to keep havering at you. We—we need you, Rom. There are things we must speak of. Will you come back with me now?"

"Yes," he said, and closed the book and got to his feet and helped her scramble up from the bank. He handed her her shoes and stockings and she carried them in her hands, feeling the warm earth with her bare feet and liking what she felt. She stopped him when they were again in sight of the caravan and repeated to him what Dr. Hay had reluctantly told her and Papa that morning. Papa, Dr. Hay had said, would never again dance upon the slack rope. He would walk again, in time, without his crutch. But the precise skill he needed for ropedancing would never come again, for the leg that was broken, though mended well enough, would always be a mite shorter than the other.

She was watching the high flight of a meadow lark as she spoke and did not see the look of panic that flicked Rom's face and was quickly gone. But she sensed trouble in his voice when he asked, "But what can we do, Polly? How will we live if he cannot—cannot . . ." He could not finish the sentence, feeling again the dismal weight of insecurity and impermanence.

"Papa and I have been talking of it," she said, after a

moment. "We have a plan and it's that we would speak of together—the three of us—now."

"What plan?" he asked, and she said, "Come along. Let Papa tell you."

Barney was sitting upon the steps of the caravan with his broken leg propped on the crutch in the sun. He grinned at them as they came up. He did not speak of the long days when Rom had fled from them, and Rom was relieved.

"You are well come, lad," Barney said as they sat on the grass at his feet. "Which of Old Will Shakespeare's tales have you been at today?"

"*Othello*, Barney. It's always been one of my favorites."

"A grim and gruesome play, to my taste, Rom. But a good enough beginning for what we have to talk of. Do you mind when Othello cries out: 'Othello's occupation's gone!' It's a saying apt to me this day, for Dr. Hay tells me I'll not dance the rope again and so my occupation's gone too. At least for a time." He tried to keep the bitterness and sense of helplessness out of his voice, but he knew he had not entirely succeeded. A ropedancer could always find a bit of money, but what chances were there for an unknown printer in a strange land?

Rom looked at him and was ashamed that he had been idling by the stream, taken up with himself, and not here when Barney needed him. He said, "Maybe the doctor's wrong, Papa," and heard himself use the old, loved term and thought how right it sounded and how stupid he'd been to boggle at it before.

Barney made no comment but some of the heaviness and discouragement had left his voice when he answered, "No, Rom. He's not wrong. I think I'd known it myself before he came, only I kept hoping for a miracle. I'll be old hop-hop-hop for the rest of my days and we might as well face it." He shook his strong, broad shoulders as if he were casting aside a burden and went on. "We'll waste no more time on that. What must be, must be. At least I'm alive

35

and that's more'n I hoped to be a few weeks gone. Fretting after what's gone and done for is nothing but a waste of good time and strength. Best take a look ahead, bairns."

"Have we—have we any money left?" Rom asked, trying to keep the despair out of his voice.

"Bless you, yes. We've enough to keep us going a while and a while. We'll not starve. Not yet. But it's best to plan for the worst, then you'll not be caught with nothing. Dr. Hay has promised to help me find work in Williamsburg, come what they call hereabouts the Public Times."

"What, under heaven, is that?" Polly put in.

"So I asked the good doctor," Barney said, and chuckled. "Simple—the answer is when you know it. Public Times are times when public business is done." He grinned at them. "Fall and spring are Public Times. Then, Dr. Hay says, yon little town that we've yet to see, comes awake. It swells to bursting point with as many folk again as are usually there. Great folk and small from all over the Colony come to attend the courts and carry on their businesses and sometimes make laws. The tobacco planters and councilors from upriver open their houses in Williamsburg. The inns and ordinaries are full and the shops do a brisk trade with special goods laid in for the time. There are balls and routs and illuminations and fairs and horse racing."

"Horse racing!" Rom forgot the purpose of this talk. "Do you suppose I could ride in a race? Do you?" He was remembering races ridden in England, especially one with another boy across the downs in a week when they had been resting and repairing their gear in an inn in the Cotswolds. The landlord had given them leave to ride his blooded horses, indeed had urged them to, since he'd been himself laid up with a sprained back and the beasts needed exercising. It had been a splendid race and Rom had loved it, as he always loved riding a great, swift horse. He thought a special knowledge of horses had been born in him and he knew he would, if given a chance, choose a

36

horse of his own over any other gift that might be his.

"Likely not, Rom," Barney said sensibly. "At least not just at first. But you can watch them, I'm sure."

"Papa!" Polly spoke sternly, bringing them back to their problem. Time enough later to think of such matters as balls and horse races.

"Well. Yes," Barney said. "Yes. The point is, Rom, Dr. Hay has promised to put in a word for me with the printer here who will likely need extra help in these Public Times. But he thinks it may be a while before I'll be up to steady work, and Polly and I have a plan for the time between. It's a plan for you and Polly which will keep our purse full enough until I can be about."

"Tell me, Papa," Rom said.

"The Little People," Barney said with the air of a magician producing a penny from Rom's ear.

"The Little People?" Rom said cautiously. He was sure the Little People had a special value and would fetch a good price if they were sold but he would rather starve than sell them. If this was what was in Papa's mind . . .

"Hear me, Rom. There's to be a biggish market here in a fortnight. What would you say to setting up the show then and, if it's liked, which it's bound to be, planning to give it regular-like during these Public Times?"

Rom considered. He was relieved that no one had suggested selling his beloved puppets, but he could see little in this notion of Papa's and Polly's. "Would people come, do you think, when we have no place indoors to give a proper showing with a proper stage? I doubt that even the Colony of Virginia is always hot?"

"And who says there'll be no place indoors?" Barney asked. "You do be a one for borrowing trouble, lad. There'll likely be a nook or a cranny we'll be welcome to use somewhere in the place, if we're ready to pay a bit of rent for it."

Rom still looked doubtful and Polly said, "Oh Rom. Don't go about being an old killjoy," and he thought since he had no better plan to suggest this was all they could do. If their purse were still as heavy as Papa had suggested it would not greatly matter anyhow. "Well, we can try," he said.

Barney reached down and gave him such a slap on his shoulder it almost sent him spinning sideways. *"That's* my lad. Now, on the morrow do you go into this Williamsburg and spy out the land and find us, if you can, a place to anchor our caravan nearer the middle of things. As Old Will Shakespeare says, 'Care killed the cat' so we'll have no more of it. What's for dinner, Polly? I'm hungry."

Rom walked the three miles to Williamsburg the next day in a heavy mood. There was, he thought, little hope that he and Polly alone could make enough to keep the three of them by showing the Little People. It had always been Papa with his magic in walking the rope with his arms, his fingers, even his nose, holding in balance an increasing number of wands and balls that had charmed the farthings and pennies from the staring crowds. The Little People, wonderful as they were, had served only to tease the onlookers and whet the appetite for the marvel to come. If they had a complete set of puppets and a real playhouse for regular performances they might succeed after a time, for he was sure there were people in the town who, like Dr. Hay, would recognize and admire the fine quality of the acting dolls. But there were only four puppets, nowhere near enough to give the elaborate shows necessary to keep a real playhouse going, and if they had to depend upon begging odd space here and there . . .

He did not bother to finish the sentence in his mind. He just didn't think they could live by the Little People, and that was that. They would have to find another way and that quickly if they weren't to starve. Last night, after Papa was snoring in his bunk, he had gotten the purse from its hiding place and counted the store of coins left and there were hardly enough to keep them a month if they had to buy their own food and likely pay somewhat for a place to keep the caravan and Betsy. Mr. Struthers had, it is true, told them to stay on as long as they liked and Mistress Struthers kept sending them food and would take no money or even thanks for it. But, with winter coming, they would be bound to be a drain upon the Struthers and, besides, Papa had said he'd not be beholden to any man for charity, no matter how kindly offered, now he was well again.

Maybe, Rom thought, he could find work. He was strong enough, though untrained. It would have been better if Papa had prenticed him back to England, instead of sending him each day to Master Popkins's school like a gentleman's son. He guessed Papa thought he was a gentleman's son, or near to it, from the fine clothes he'd been found in, and had wanted to make up to him for all he'd lost. Gentleman's son, indeed! Son, rather, to a scurvy actor eager to be rid of his children. '*Be rid of them—both of them—and that right quickly.*'

He must not think of the letter, for it would only anger him and distract his mind from what must be done this day.

The trees of the forest that stretched on each side of the road were thinning, and he looked ahead and came to a handsome building and walked faster around it until he could see ahead a broad straight roadway and along each side the cheerful houses and shops, the inns and ordinaries and the gardens of Williamsburg, capital of the Colony of Virginia. He stood, for a moment, looking toward the town, quiet in the morning sun. There were few people about and those he could see were taking their ease. A man in a plain white shirt and dark red breeches under a leather apron was smoking a clay pipe in a doorway along the road a piece. He wore a skullcap and Rom could see that his right shoulder and right foot were larger than the left and he knew this was a pressman who had overdeveloped the one side with the heavy work of pulling his

39

press. For a moment Rom was almost blinded with home-sickness, remembering his good friend the pressman in the shop at Petersfield, and he jumped when he felt a hand on his shoulder and heard a gruff but kindly voice at his side.

"Morning, boy. You're a stranger here, I'm thinking. Least I've not seen you before to my knowledge and I know every man and boy in the town. Are you come to the College, then?"

"College, sir?" Rom asked.

"Aye." The man gestured along the roadway ahead of them. "The College of William and Mary there at the other end of the town."

"No, sir. I'm seeking a place where we, my—my father and my sister and I, can keep our caravan."

"So that's it. You belong to the ropedancer that took a fall and broke a leg and was like to die of it. Poor fellow. I do hope he is well recovered."

"He is, sir, I thank you. But—but how did you know about it?"

"Why, easily, boy. From my friend, Dr. Hay. There's little goes on in this town doesn't come to my ears soon or late. So you're wanting to leave Struthers's meadow and come closer to the middle of things are you? Good. Good. It's a sensible notion. Do you just go along yon Duke of Gloucester Street you can see there before you—*if* you can see it properly for the infernal dust—how we do need rain—till you come to the Palace Green. You'll know it right enough, with the Governor's House all fair and fit again at the end. Then do you go up to the Palace gate and turn smart right and follow the road till you come to a post-mill. There's land aplenty wasting round it. Do you tell the miller your needs and tell him John Blair sent you. You'll not forget the name, boy?"

"No, sir, Mr. Blair. . . ."

"Councilor, boy, councilor. Councilor John Blair."

"Yes, sir. I'll not forget. Councilor John Blair, and thank you, sir."

40

"Thrice welcome, boy. What's your name?"

"Hormsby, sir. Romulus Hormsby."

"Romulus Hormsby, is it? It's a good name, a right good name. Pity you've not got a twin brother named Remus."

"It is, sir, for that would make us proper Romans. But I do have a twin sister named Polly. I reckon she'll have to do," Rom said, and grinned at the kindly gentleman.

John Blair threw back his head and roared with laughter. He put his hand on Rom's shoulder and gave him a gentle push and said, "Well, get along with you, boy. I've my work to do in the Capitol yonder."

Rom said, "It's a fine building, sir. I thank you again for your kind help," and started up the Duke of Gloucester Street toward the Palace Green. Blair watched him go a moment, muttering to himself, "A good face, though overtroubled for a lad. Good bones behind it. Wish I could say who he puts me in mind of. Somebody hereabouts or my memory's going. Good mind, too. Should be in the College. Well, not your business, John Blair." He watched Rom's back a moment longer and turned away toward the Capitol.

Rom walked along the street past an ordinary, past the goldsmith's and the step where the pressman had stood for his smoke—yes it was a print shop as he had guessed—past houses and stores and storehouses and gardens, his feet rustling in the first fallen leaves from the young trees that lined the roadway. He passed a great brick house with steps leading right and left up to a stone doorstep and a glimpse of dwarf box bushes beyond a white paling fence, passed another tavern with a bowling green beside it and a wide square where sheep grazed, and came at last to a long plaza bordered by trees he could not name. At its end stood a graceful, wide-winged building flanked by smaller buildings and guarded by a low brick wall and great iron gates topped with the Arms of England. Councilor Blair had been right. No one could mistake the

Palace Green and the stately Governor's House at its end.

Rom took the marl-filled path that skirted the Green and ran before other gracious houses and gardens, larger for the most part than those on the Duke of Gloucester Street, and turned right at its end and came to the mill set high upon a post, its sails turned to catch the breeze coming lightly out of the west. There was, as the Councilor had promised, plenty of ground, grass-covered and empty, about the mill and Rom thought this would be a fine place for their caravan.

He came up to the mill and shouted, to be heard above the turning of the sails, for the miller. A great, tousled head appeared for a moment at the door and a great voice shouted down to Rom, "Come up, then, boy, come up and say your business for the miller can no come down when the corn's a-grinding."

Rom climbed the short, steep ladder to the mill and went into its cool dusty interior and, shouting still, told the miller his business, mentioning that Councilor John Blair had sent him.

The miller, his back to Rom, made an adjustment to his stones. He poured a sack of wheat kernels into the hopper and waited to see that the grain was running smoothly.

Rom waited, too, soothed by the half-lit interior of the place and by the clatter, *clump*, clatter, *clump* of the sails and the clash of the iron teeth engaging as the stones turned and the rattle of the wheat in the hopper. He hoped the miller had heard his request and wondered whether he should offer payment or wait to be asked for it.

The miller, satisfied the new run was going properly, turned to him and said, "Yon Councilor Blair's a good man. He's helped me many's the time and I'm glad to do a favor for him for the once. Sure and you can put your—caravan, did you call it?—in yon meadow and pasture your horse to boot. Save me scything the grass, most like. I've heard

42

of your misfortune and it will pleasure me to be of service to you."

Rom thought everybody seemed to know all about them. "It's kind of you, sir," he began, but the miller cut him short, laughing. "I'm no sir, lad. Just plain Ben Post is good enough for me. Glad to have you, glad to have you. When will I expect you, then?"

"Could we—would tomorrow be too soon, if we can manage by then?"

"Any time you like, lad. Meadow's not going to move away. Any time you like. It will be a fine thing to have folk about when the wind's slack and the sail's not turning and no need for any soul to come to mill. Oops!"

He jumped back to the stones as he caught some change in the tempo of their sound too slight for Rom's ears. "Come then tomorrow or when you will," he called over his shoulder. "And mind the sails when you go out. They be onery creatures when they've a mind. Their tips go a mighty pace in a good wind and even in this middling breeze they're like to give you a buffet you'll not soon forget should you get in their path."

He feels about his sails as I do about my Little People —as if they were alive—Rom thought. He was going to like the miller. He started back toward the Palace Green.

CHAPTER FIVE

An hour later Rom trudged down a lane between two houses, his head bent, his hands held tight at his sides. He had left the miller feeling sure things were going well for the Hormsbys. All he had to do now was find among the shops or ordinaries someone who needed a willing boy to run errands or the like and he would have a splendid tale to take back to Polly and Papa. He had started confidently upon his rounds, stepping out quickly, sure that this was his lucky day and nothing could go amiss.

And now . . .

Discouragement sat upon his shoulders and mocked hope. He had been up one side of the town and down the other. He had begged for work—any work—from the boot and shoemaker, the goldsmith, the tailor, the wigmaker; from John Holt who sold everything from lengths of cloth to wine and tea, and from the cabinetmaker. He had asked at the stately Raleigh Tavern and Well's Ordinary and at Mrs. Charleton's. And everywhere he had found the same answer. Nobody needed a helper now. Nobody would promise work later. Some said, maybe—if the Public Times brought good business. Come back again in two month's time.

Two months. By then it would be too late. They could starve in two months, he and Papa and Polly. He wondered if he might find someone who would take him as a prentice and discarded the thought for it would not help Polly and Papa. He would get no wages as a prentice, only bed and board, clothes, and the chance to learn a trade. There was nothing left but the Little People. If they failed to bring in enough for food . . .

"Watch where you're going, stupid oaf!"

The words stopped Rom's blundering feet in their tracks. He looked up and saw the speaker, a boy about his own age, heavyset, with strong, coarse features and straight, thick black hair that hung loose about his shoulders and needed cutting. He was standing in front of a kind of box, scowling, as if he wanted to keep its contents secret. His little eyes, almost hidden between straight, thick brows and a roll of flesh that made the lower eyelid, gleamed with illwill from a face white as an uncooked pasty. "Who do you think you are, blundering along where you're not wanted, you scurvy rat?"

Rom was in no condition of mind to take this rude name-calling calmly. But the boy looked dangerous, and Rom felt his stomach begin to churn with the old fear of fighting. He looked at the boy's great, rough hands and felt the flesh of his face quiver and shrink as he imagined the feel of their impact upon it. He swallowed the wrath rising in him and spoke softly, "I—I crave your pardon. I did not know this was a private place."

The boy moved into the middle of the lane, forgetting to cover what he had been hiding and Rom saw it was a crude, badly built puppet theater, its opening framed by a ragged gray cloth which did duty as a curtain. Lying on the floor of the stage were two bedraggled dolls, their heads hacked rather than carved from a piece of rough pine wood. Rom guessed by their shabby costumes they were supposed to be Punch and his Judy.

Rom laughed. The laugh came partly from his stretched nerves and partly because, as he thought of the puppet stage he and Papa had made so lovingly and beautifully from cedar wood for the Little People, this caricature seemed to him at the very least amusing.

The black-haired boy moved closer to him, until his face was no more than six inches away, and raised his hands menacingly. "Laugh at my show, will you? You'll not laugh long then, Master High and Mighty. Nobody laughs long at Black Rafe Bascomb. Those do be my practice puppets, but someday I aim to have a real show and then we'll see who laughs!"

Rom said, forgetting to be cautious, "You'll never have a decent show if you're satisfied with that, even for practice. Nor yet till you learn somewhat of carving faces that look like faces. You should see some *real* puppets."

"Likely you'll show them to me," Black Rafe said softly.

"Likely I will, do you but come to the Market Square when you see our caravan there."

Black Rafe's eyes grew stubborn. "Those puppets yonder are as good as any in the world," he said.

Rom laughed again.

Black Rafe drew in his breath with a long, hissing sound. "Do you want I should prove it?" he asked, and Rom remembered suddenly how frightened he was and knew his fear showed in his eyes. He took a step backward and tried to get around Rafe in the narrow lane.

Rafe shifted to keep him where he was. "Will you put up your hands and fight like a man?" His mouth spread into a sly grin though his eyes were hard and cold. "Or will you ask my pardon and *say my show's as good as ever you saw?*"

Rom mumbled, "I ask your pardon. Now will you step aside and let me pass?"

Rafe did not move. "Not until you say 'Your show's as good as ever I saw!'" he said.

Rom gulped. It wasn't true and he could not say it. No matter what happened he would not say it. To say it would be a disloyalty and a dishonor to the Little People. But he could not fight either. There must be some way. There must be.

"Well," Rafe said, "make up your mind!" His mean eyes were laughing. Rom thought: He knows I'm afraid and he's enjoying it. He's taking his time, playing with me. But another part of his mind was trying to see a way out of the situation.

"Stand back, then," he said. "If you're so anxious to fight, give me room."

He balanced himself on the balls of his feet and held his body tight. If he could just get this Rafe off balance for one minute he could run away from him, he was sure. He hated himself for the thought and watched Rafe's eyes.

He saw laughter go out of them, chased away by surprise and by something else Rom could not define, though it seemed for a moment as if Rafe were himself afraid. Rafe took one step backward and Rom moved. He jumped forward, but a little to the left, and started to run, giving Rafe a hard shove as he passed. Rafe stumbled, regained his balance, and let out a roar of anger. He started after Rom shouting, "Come back here, you filthy little coward, you sneak, you scoundrel. Come back here and take the beating that's coming to you."

The lane seemed endless. Rom was breathing hard and his legs felt as if he had hundredweights for feet. The long days on shipboard and the other days of nursing Papa had, he guessed desperately, taken strength from his muscles and sapped his wind. He had thought he could outrun anybody, certainly anybody as heavyset as Black Rafe, but he heard pounding feet coming closer and closer and fear dragged at him and he slowed still more. He wondered which way he should turn at the lane's end and, wondering, came to the end and felt Rafe's hands at his back trying to hold him. He jerked himself forward and Rafe, though he missed his hold, managed to thrust at him and he hurtled out into the dust of the Duke of Gloucester Street. He heard the beat of a horse's hooves coming at a gallop and a voice yelling curses and felt a hot wind pass not six inches from his head.

He lay in the dust, dazed, not sure for a moment whether he had been trampled by the horseman or not. He moved his legs and arms cautiously and found them whole and lifted his head expecting to see Rafe coming after him, but Black Rafe had disappeared.

Rom pulled himself upright and got slowly to his feet. Far down the street near the College, a rider was still struggling to control his frightened horse. There was no other human being in sight. Across from him the Market Square slept in the noonday sun and the sheep cropped the yellow goldenrod in the drought-dried grass.

He got out of the roadway and limped toward the Capitol and the road that would take him home to the caravan. There was a stream on the way. He would drink from it and wash the dust from his hands and face before he came to Polly and Papa. He would not tell them of Rafe or his own cowardice. He hated himself because he had not dared to fight.

He skirted the Capitol and came into the road through the forest and, at last, to the stream. He lay full length beside it and cupped the cool water in his hands and drank again and again. When his thirst was satisfied he splashed his face until it felt cool and clean and brushed his shirt and breeches with a pine branch to rid them of the road dust.

He was tired clear through to his bones. He would just rest a little. He lay upon the pine needles and tried to forget the things that had happened to him this day. The warm smell of the pines, the running trill of the stream, the sleepy noontime noises of birds, lulled him and, for a while, he slept.

He woke slowly, conscious of a lump that pressed into his side, and twisted to get away from it. The movement brought him wide-awake, and he put his hand in the pocket of his breeches and brought out a packet of wild ginger root Mistress Struthers had given him when he left, asking him to exchange it at the apothecary's for horehound drops for her youngest child, who had a worrisome cough. He had clean forgot her errand.

He would have to go back. He had promised to bring her the medicine. He could not fail her after all her kindness to them.

He felt the fear turning in his stomach. What if he should come again upon Black Rafe? He could not go back. He could not.

But he must.

He told himself Rafe would not dare set upon him in the apothecary shop nor yet in the public streets, but his fear did not go away. Yet he must go. He set his teeth and got up and turned back into the road to town, hurrying a little, thinking the sooner his errand were done the quicker he would be safe again.

The apothecary shop smelled of cloves and cinnamon, perfumes and pomades, and licorice whips. Two men in plain linen stocks, dark breeches, and brown wigs were talking to a clerk. A third man stood beside great glass bottles filled with blue and red liquid. He leaned over the broad counter reading a copy of *The Virginia Gazette* spread upon it. Rom, feeling less afraid here, stopped looking over his shoulder and stood beside the reader, waiting patiently until a clerk would be free to attend to him. No one seemed to be in a hurry. No one seemed to notice him, and he was content to wait.

He could, by shifting a little, see clearly a section of the *Gazette* and, without consciously intending it, he began to read what he could see, and summarize it in his mind.

The Greyhound, *Captain Davis, had anchored four days previously from Africa, with 400 slaves consigned to Hill and Rootes; and the sloop,* Virginia, *had come into the York River on August 14 from Philadelphia, with rum and sugar, wine, molasses, chocolate, coffee, soap, and limes.*

Rom wondered how chocolate tasted. It had a good, rich sound.

50

Three days ago the Briton *of Whitehaven had sailed again for her home port with John Harrison as Captain and, as cargo, 361 hogsheads of tobacco, 6,000 staves, 1,000 feet of plank, and 14 tons of pig iron.*

Rom wished with all his heart he were sailing in her. He'd be on his way to England—on his way home to a safe and secure place, to a place of permanence, to fields and lanes he knew and loved.

One Ambrose Bullock of Spotsylvania County had, at his plantation, a strayed mare. She was small and black, with a hanging mane and long tail. She was branded on the near buttock, and her owner could have her of Bullock on proving his property and paying as the law directs.

Rom hoped the little mare was being well cared for. There was something about her hanging mane and long tail that appealed to him and he wished he might have her.

Two servants of Robert Stobo had run away. Both were Englishmen. One, Thomas Fermy, was a tailor and wore, when he left, a coarse gray jacket, a striped holland shirt, osnaburg trousers, and a pair of new shoes. The other was James Croson, who was pitted with smallpox and also had on a pair of new shoes.

Probably bond servants of an unkind master, Rom thought, pitying them and wondering if they had waited for the new shoes before escaping.

The man beside him moved the paper, and Rom's eyes shifted focus. "By permission of the Honorable Robert Dinwiddie, Esq., His Majesty's Lieutenant-Governor," he read, "by a Company of Comedians, from London, at the Theater in Williamsburg, on Friday next, being the 15th of September, will be presented a play called *The Merchant of Venice* (written by Shakespeare). The part of Antonio (the Merchant) to be performed by Mr. Clarkson, Gratiano by Mr. Singleton, Lorenzo (with songs in character) by Mr. Adcock, the part of . . ."

"Sorry to have kept you waiting, sir. Your potion took a deal of pounding."

A second clerk spoke as he came through a door at the back of the shop and the man beside Rom picked up the *Gazette* and shook its sheets into place. Rom continued to stare at the place where the paper had been. His heart was pounding and thumping with excitement. A Theater! Right here in Williamsburg! And doing one of Old Will Shakespeare's plays! And he'd not known it. Papa was right. He did know most of the plays by heart —or the best parts of them at any rate. But he'd never seen one of them acted by real, live men and women. He and Polly had sometimes done scenes for their own amusement with the Little People. But that was hardly the same thing. Dearly as he loved the Little People they weren't the same as real, live actors. And besides, Polly nearly always got the lines mixed up.

He wondered where the Theater was, how much a ticket in the gallery would cost. He'd have to find some way to get there. He'd *have* to. He'd . . .

"Are you deaf, young sir?" The clerk who had come from the back was plucking at his sleeve and shouting at him. Rom shook his head and looked at the clerk, tongue-tied with embarrassment as he saw everyone in the shop watching him and smiling.

"Come along now," the clerk went on, kindly enough, "We've no time to spend while you gather wool. How can I serve you?"

Rom laid the packet of wild ginger roots on the counter. "Horehound, sir, if it please you. In exchange. It's for Mistress Struthers."

"Ah, then, you must be the son of yon ropedancer fell and near lost his life from poison in the blood."

Rom nodded. Did everybody in Williamsburg know all about them?

"Wild ginger," the clerk went on, emptying the contents of the packet first into the pan of a scales on a shelf at his back and then into a blue and gray earthenware jar beside him. From another jar he took a doublehandful of horehound drops and wrapped them in a sheet of newsprint and handed Rom the parcel. "Horehound, is it? The young one must have a phlegm in him. Tell Mistress Struthers to keep him quiet and feed him light. And here's a licorice whip for you, lad. You're right welcome to our Williamsburg and may your luck turn again soon."

Rom mumbled his thanks and fled from the still amused eyes of the clerks and patrons. These were kind people, most of them, but he wished they didn't all know so much about him. He looked fearfully along the street, half expecting to see Black Rafe lurking somewhere, waiting for him. A farm cart driven by an elderly Negro in a faded blue shirt ambled slowly along the middle of the roadway. Two women with wickerwork baskets of red and white carnations and blue phlox talked together across a white paling fence between their two gardens. A group of young men from the College, their black gowns flapping, walked slowly, talking seriously. There was nothing out of the ordinary, no menacing black head and squinched-up eyes to mar the peace of the day. Rom headed once more, almost running, toward the forest road and safety. When he was a mile from town he remembered he was hungry and ate the licorice whip.

It was nearly sundown when he came to the caravan, and he noticed with surprise how the days were drawing in, making way for the early autumn dark. Papa was sitting on the steps, enjoying the last of the sun. He got up heavily, leaning on his crutch as Rom turned from the farm road into the field. "You've been a long time gone, lad," he said. "I'd begun to fret about you, thinking you'd lost yourself in yon Williamsburg. Is it a good town, do you think?"

"Yes," Rom said, "likely a good town, though overquiet now. It will be lively enough later they say. I forgot Mistress Struthers's horehound until I was partway home and had to go back for it. It was that made me late."

He hoped that would explain the time he had taken.

He wanted no questions from Papa. He would not speak of Rafe, and he did not want to confess his failure to find work. Barney seemed satisfied, for he nodded. "Then you'd best take it to her straightaway. She'll be needing it most like. But do you not tarry overlong."

"I'll not. I'm fair swooning with hunger."

He went along to the house and gave Mistress Struthers the horehound and the clerk's message about caring for the sick child. Mistress Struthers sniffed. "You'd think Will Johnson was a real doctor then, stead of a pothecary's prentice," she said. "As if I'd not learned to care for a cough and me with ten sons and daughters alive and strong from the twelve I've borne these twelve years past. Thank you, Rom, for bringing the horehound. I will say for Will Johnson he gave me good measure. I'll be churning on the morrow. Do you or Mistress Polly come along for a bit of butter and a jug of buttermilk. There's nothing like the buttermilk for putting strength into a man after a fever."

Rom thanked her and went back to the caravan. Polly had spread a cloth and set out a loaf of bread and thick slices of cold mutton and a jug of milk. Papa wanted to start in at once questioning Rom about the day, but Rom said, "Please, Papa. I'm much too hungry to talk. I've had nothing but a licorice whip since morning," and Papa said, "Fall to, then, lad, and be quick about it for I'm as full of curiosity as you are of hunger."

They finished their supper as the last of the sunset flamed green and gold in the west. Polly cleared the remains of the meal quickly and brought the stools for herself and Rom, while Barney settled himself and his crutch once more on the steps.

Rom told them then of such part of his day as he wished them to know. He told of meeting Councilor Blair and of the miller who would gladly, for the companionship they would bring him, have them and their caravan and Betsy settled upon the field by his mill. Barney said then, "Good,

54

Rom. That's better than I'd hoped. When I've work to do again we'll manage to pay the good miller for the use of his land, but it's well to know we can take our time about it. When can we move?"

"When we are ready. Tomorrow if we like."

He told them then about the town—the shops and houses, the Governor's Palace, and the Capitol. Polly wanted to know more of the shops and Barney of the printers and Rom answered their questions patiently, keeping till the last his news of the Theater.

When they ran out of questions he said quietly, "I found out something else while I was waiting for Mistress Struthers's horehound. There's a Theater in Williamsburg and a company of Comedians from London who are going to play Old Will Shakespeare's *Merchant of Venice* on the fifteenth of September."

"Glory!" Barney shouted, thumping his crutch in his excitement. "That's a packet of news, and you wait till the last and tell it as if you were talking about the weather. You'll be there, Rom, you and Polly sitting in a box as grand as the next."

Rom laughed. "The gallery will do as well, Papa, and be a sight less dear."

The laughter died. He would not tell Papa he doubted they'd have enough coins in their purse to buy even one seat in the gallery. Barney saw the doubt and started to speak, but Polly was ahead of him. "Rom! Papa! If this Company of Comedians is newly come from London maybe our—maybe *Patrick Malone* is with them."

The thought struck Rom as if it had been a stone hurled at him. In all the day in the town he had given no thought to Patrick Malone or the hateful letter. Not even the news of the Theater had brought it to his mind. Polly's suggestion brought back the letter now and all its power to hurt him. His pleasure in the Theater vanished and he sank again into the hole of misery from which he'd only recently taken so long a time to climb.

He wished he had not read the notice, wished they could go quickly away from this place and never come back. He only half-heard Barney saying, "Hush you, Polly. Have you no wits? There's no cause to think such a thing. Come, we'd best go within, for the dark's come down and we've much to do if we are to move on the morrow. Rom, lend me your shoulder to lean on. This blasted crutch is an awkward thing."

Rom did not move. Barney leaned toward him and grasped his shoulder and shook it. Rom winced with pain that reached inside his despair and roused him. He must have bruised that shoulder badly when he fell in the road.

"Rom!" Barney spoke sharply, almost as if he were angry. "I asked your help. Must I beg you for it?"

Rom moved quickly, ashamed because his ears had been stopped by hate and anger, not blaming Papa. But Barney said softly, gently as Rom got him to his feet, "Do not fret, Romulus, it will come right in time. You'll see."

CHAPTER SIX

Market Day was high and blue and shimmering with a golden haze that hung about Williamsburg, making it into a town of faerie. Rain, in the week just passed, had come softly and lasted for three days, scouring away the dust and bringing new life to the tired, brown grass. A day of sun and mild breezes after the downpour had dried the mud puddles and left the air singing and tingling with the smell of autumn.

Before daylight, at the edge of the Market Square, Rom and Polly, with Barney standing by, leaning lightly upon his crutch, had set up their puppet theater on the tailgate of the caravan. There had been an argument about what play they would choose for the Little People. Polly, as usual, had wanted to do *The History of Dr. Faustus* so they could use the royal robe that had been with the puppets from the very beginning. It was a loose cloak of rich black velvet, cunningly made to hide the rods which brought the Little People to life, or seemed to, and it had upon the back, finely worked in threads of scarlet and gold, a curious symbol—a T supporting an egg-shaped loop. A gypsy man they had met at a fair had told them the strange device was called the Ankh and was an ancient Egyptian symbol of life. Whether he was right they did not know, but Polly loved the robe the more after that and was forever begging to show the King Puppet in it. It set off the King's fine, strong face, she said.

More often than not Rom was willing enough to use a play that called for the special robe, but today he had argued against it. He did not think that any of the plays in which they could use it were right for Market Day. People who came to market to sell or to buy were not in serious mood. They did not want to see plays about high matters. They wanted to be entertained. He had said, weighing the thin purse in his hand to give the more point to his argument, they could take no chances with their audience today. Papa was getting stronger, but Dr. Hay would not say how soon he'd be fit to work and they needed every coin they could wheedle out of the crowd of sellers and buyers from the town and the nearby countryside. Even more important, they needed to please the people who came to watch them, please them so much they would go away singing praises for the Little People so others would hear and come to the next show and the next. Better do *Dick Whittington and His Cat*. Everybody liked that.

Polly, reluctantly, had agreed, and so the Little People, dressed in the appropriate costumes Polly had made for them, were set in their grooves on the stage floor, ready to do their parts under the quick and clever hands of their owners.

Rom looked at Polly critically. She had on a spangly

dress hurriedly pieced together from Papa's best costumes. He would never use them again, he had said, and she'd best do what she could with them rather than waste the good materials for sentiment's sake. She held in front of her a scroll lettered large in red from the juice of poke-berries the miller had showed them how to squeeze into ink. The scroll announced that the famous Hormsby Giant

Puppets, direct from England, would show each hour throughout the day, at the end of the Market Square nearest the Palace Green, the well-known play, *Dick Whittington and His Cat.*

Beside Polly stood a small boy in a long red surcoat and a green turban. He held a little drum from their property chest. He tapped it gently, now and then, and his even, white teeth showed in a wide grin. He was son to the cook at the Palace and had jumped up and down with pleasure when Rom asked last week if he would beat the drum to announce their show to the town on Market Day.

"You'll do, Pol," Rom said. "And you'd best get on with it. You know where you're going?"

"Of course, Rom. Stop fretting."

"Say it again. I want to be sure you've got it *right.*"

Polly sighed, and looked at Barney. "Best say it again, lass. Our Rom must ever be sure of everybody's lines."

"Up the Duke of Gloucester Street to the College and around Prince George Street to the Palace Green. By Scotland Street to North England Street and thence to Nicholson Street. Down Nicholson Street to the Capitol and up the Duke of Gloucester Street and back to you."

"Very good. Now be off with you."

Rom gave the boy a pat on the shoulder. "And do you, William George, rattle your drum right smartly so all will know where to look for us."

William George struck his drum and stepped out with Polly following two paces behind him. She stopped at once and said, "But Rom I feel so—so *silly* doing this. Do you go in my stead," and Rom gave her a little push and a frown. "Don't make a fuss, Polly. People will always look at a dressed-up girl. Nobody would pay any mind to me. Now do go *on.*"

He watched her as she hurried to catch up with her drummer. Her hair shone golden in the sun and her back was straight and tall as she marched. She was, he thought, a pretty girl all right, especially in the spangly dress. He was proud of her though he'd not tell her so. He hoped they would drum up a real crowd for the show.

He stared across the Duke of Gloucester Street at the powder magazine. The guard were making ready to fire the morning gun. The sergeant thrust a long, lighted match into the breech and fired. Black smoke billowed out from the cannon's mouth and a hollow roar, thin and without resonance, drifted across the Square.

Rom turned back to see Polly and William George marching bravely into Nicholson Street. Distantly he could hear the drumbeats. A few people seemed to be watching. He wondered if anybody would come to see them. He wished they could begin. He hated waiting.

Barney said, "Ease down, Rom. No use running to meet trouble that likely won't come."

Barney had begun to feel more comfortable in his mind about Rom this past week. For a time the black mood that had come upon him with Polly's ill-considered reminder of Patrick Malone had kept him silent and miserable. He had gone about the business of moving the caravan to the mill field as if his mind had left him, though his movements were as neat and efficient as they always were. Once they were settled in their new place he had, at first, spent most of his time with Betsy and a book, or had hung about the mill helping the miller turn the great lumbering structure upon its post to bring the sails into the wind or watching him grind the corn and wheat.

There was another thing that had troubled Barney. Rom kept looking over his shoulder as if he had feared something or somebody and, when questioned about it gently and kindly, had flown in anger and gone away.

It was Polly who had finally brought him out of his mood. She had waited one day until he had done with turning the mill and called him urgently as if she were ill or hurt and he had come running fast enough. He had been furious when he found her smiling and safe, but she had given his fury no space to spend itself. She had spoken first and showed him the rough side of her tongue right enough and shamed him into his due part in making ready the puppets and their theater for Market Day. Strange about Rom. You'd never drive him to anything, but you could always shame him into doing what was right.

Since then he'd been more himself, though he still scowled frequently and looked now and then behind him as if he were afeared. Today he had evidently forgotten everything except the Little People and the show they were to give.

God grant the show would be successful. If they failed to fill the tambourine when he passed it Barney didn't know what they would do. He didn't need Rom to tell him how empty their purse was. He had tried going about a bit without his crutch and while he could make it for a step or two he was still far from strong in the leg. He sighed and saw Polly and William George passing the Bowling Green and pulled himself straight and fixed upon his face the smile he was finding it harder and harder to keep in place.

Rom poked his head out from between the folds of their red velvet curtain. The curtain was painted with a scene from some ancient play and had been in the box with the Little People when they were first discovered. Rom's head looked overlarge, like a giant's, framed in the small arch of the puppet theater. "Where *is* Polly, Papa?" he asked irritably. "There's a plenty of people about already. We should begin."

"Patience," Barney said, "she's but a little distance off. She'll be here in a bit. Are the Little People ready?"

"And waiting in their grooves. All we need is Polly." Rom withdrew his head and let the curtain fall into place.

Polly crossed the Market Square, threading her way among the booths set up for vegetables and the pens where sheep and cattle baa'd and bawled, poultry cackled, and mammoth hogs, fattened on corn and acorns until they could scarcely stand, grunted and squealed. She dodged half-a-dozen children playing with a ball and stopped to look curiously at an Indian in buckskin trousers and a red soldier's coat making his way toward one of the booths. Barney cupped his hands and called to her and beckoned her to hurry.

William George came, puffing a little, behind her. He beat a final rat-a-tat on his drum and bobbed his thanks again and again when Barney gave him a shilling for his services. "Run along home now, William George," Barney ordered him, "afore your mam starts fretting." The small boy looked at Polly appealingly and Polly said, "Let him stay to see the show, Papa. His mam won't miss him yet. Besides, I promised William George."

"Do you sit here then beside me, boy, and mind you keep still," Barney said, and William George plumped his fat body on the ground beside Barney's crutch tip and did not move.

A small crowd of people, women mostly and their children, came across the Square. They edged their way crabwise, in ones and twos, each group hanging back as if none wanted to be first to arrive. Barney leaned against the caravan for support and raised his crutch and beckoned them on with it. "Come one, come all," he shouted, "come and see the giant Hormsby Puppets, fresh from England. See the Little People. Hear them speak. Watch them move. Come along, good people, and watch the greatest marvel of our age."

A dozen people stood before the caravan, looking sheepish as if they wondered why they were here. They were plainly dressed though Barney guessed they'd worn their best clothes for Market Day. He sighed, thinking there'd likely not be a pistole between them when he took the tambourine around after the show. He wished for the thousandth time he could be dancing upon the rope. That would fetch them, he'd dare swear. If only in the hope— some of them, anyway—to see him fall. Well, he'd had his first fall and his last, and now it was up to the young ones and the Little People. Maybe there'd be more lookers later, if the stalls and booths did good business. If this batch gave a good account of the show. There'd be no more now. So much was clear, and they'd best begin.

He picked up the tambourine from the edge of the caravan and lifted it high and rattled it as a signal to Rom and Polly. He pulled the cord that opened the red velvet curtain and felt somewhat cheered as the little crowd drew in its breath to see the stage and a miniature Dick Whittington sitting disconsolate against a miniature milepost with his miniature cat beside him. They were proud of that cat, for they had made him themselves and they knew he was good.

"Alas! Alas!"

Rom's voice from behind the curtain that masked the back of the stage was filled with woe. He moved his hands swiftly, turning the rod that controlled the puppet's head and Dick Whittington sank his head into his hands for all the world as if he were alive.

"Ah-h-h-h-h," the audience sighed.

"Meow!" Polly spoke for the cat, and the cat moved closer and appeared to rub against Whittington's legs.

William George stood up, the better to see the stage, and began inching nearer to it. His eyes were huge and shining with excitement. He kept saying, "Lordy! Lordy!" under his breath. The watching people unconsciously followed his lead and moved up a step or two, and Barney relaxed. Rom and Polly and the Little People had cast their spell. The little crowd would give whatever they could when the show was done. Better still, they would go away and tell others who would come later. They should have a good, heavy purse before the day was out. Heavy enough, please heaven, to see them through, with care, until he could find work for himself; for, though he would never admit it to Rom and Polly, he had little faith in the ability of the puppets to make them a living on any long-time basis. But once he had his hands on a printing press he'd warrant he'd keep the job, Public Times or no Public Times, and he had, at least, a hope he'd be given this work he knew so well.

He looked over the Square, filling rapidly with the people of the town; tavern keepers making for the animal pens, ladies with servants following, children darting and running between their elders and threatening to upset them, shouting good naturedly. Two gentlemen in bright coats and carefully tended wigs started across the Square from the Market Tavern, talking with wide gestures. One was tall and slender, the other shorter and stouter. But the tall, slender one seemed to defer always to the other. Barney wondered who they were as the shorter man turned toward the Capitol.

The other put his hand on his companion's arm and pointed in the direction of the caravan. They talked for a second, then reversed their steps and came on across the Square toward the puppet show.

A black-haired, hulking boy who had been following them at a little distance turned with them, looked where they looked, stared with his mouth open, and began to run heavily after them. As the two men stopped a little to one side of the caravan their pursuer came up behind one of the women in the audience and plucked at her sleeve.

Barney stiffened. Now what in the name of Old Will Shakespeare and all his plays was going on? He wanted to go to the boy and ask him to leave, but he did not like to interrupt the performance. Perhaps the thing, whatever it was, would straighten itself out.

The woman tried to shake off the hand, but the boy began to whisper in her ear and, after a moment, she grabbed an arm of each of two children with her and hurried them away in spite of their protests. The small commotion had broken in upon the concentration of the rest of the audience and they turned from the stage and gaped at the boy, who was speaking now to the woman next nearest him. She, like the first, hurried away, drawing her skirts about her as if she feared to dirty them. The black-haired boy, seeing he had the attention of all the others, put his finger to his lips and started back toward the center of the Square, beckoning them, and they, without another glance at the puppets, followed until only William George and the two gentlemen were left.

Barney felt as if the world had, of a sudden, turned mad. What could that devil-sent boy have said? This would surely ruin all their hopes and chances. He heard Polly's voice behind the curtain falter and miss a line and heard Rom pick up the next line loud and clear to cover her lapse. Stout lad, Barney thought. So long as there's anyone to watch he'll finish the job.

Polly, after her one faltering, took the next cue as if nothing had happened and together they finished the play. The Little People, Barney thought, responded as if they did indeed have life and voices and wills of their own and wished to help in this emergency. Not a rod moved but smoothly and quietly, though at times they stuck or jerked as if the devil himself were in them. They had never done so fine a show and when the last line had been said he closed the curtains with a flourish and bowed over his crutch to William George as if the lone boy had been five hundred cheering and clapping people.

He had forgotten the two gentlemen. He was surprised when he heard them applauding as loudly as they could, as if they would make up for the lack of other applause, and saw them crossing the grass to him.

As they came abreast of him, Polly and Rom burst through the red curtain, their faces forlorn and angry. "Oh, Papa!" Polly said, near breaking into tears. "What happened? I thought I should die when all the people went away. What did we do wrong? I've never felt so shamed."

Before Barney could answer, the shorter of the two men spoke, "Nay, mistress. You've no cause for shame. On the contrary. It was none of your doing. Some rascal—we could not see him clearly for he kept himself well-hidden behind your audience, though whether by design or accident I do not know—some rascal from the town, I'd guess, drew away the watchers with a tale to frighten or anger them. I've seen the like done before but never more cleverly."

Rom's stomach drew into a knot. He knew who had spoiled their show, knew in his bones it was Black Rafe. Who else would have cause to do them hurt—to do him hurt? Who else . . .

67

"But how?" Polly had turned to the two gentlemen. "And why?"

"Who can say, mistress?"—the stranger moved his shoulders—"but it is sure you've no cause to blame yourself. You've reason rather to be proud for there's many an actor far older and more experienced than you would not have had the courage to finish the play in the face of such odds."

"Thank—thank you, sir," Polly said. She was wondering what had come over Rom. His face had lost all its color and he was shaking as if he had an ague.

"And now, sir"—the stranger turned to Barney—"do you intend to be here in Williamsburg long?"

"We are not idly curious," the taller man put in quickly, as Barney hesitated over his reply, "we have good cause to ask."

"Bless you, sirs," Barney said. "I've no objection to your question. In truth I scarce know how to answer it." He tried to smile at Polly and Rom but this time the smile would not stay in place. "I'm Barnabas Hormsby, sirs." The two men looked at one another and nodded. "Late a ropedancer in England."

The tall man started to speak, but the other put his hand on his arm, stopping him, and Barney went on: "I had hoped to do a bit of dancing here in the Colonies until this"—he pointed with his crutch to his shortened leg— "put an end to it. Now—well, sirs, it should be a time and a time the doctor says before I should try to move on again and we had hoped to stay here and eke out a living with the Little People."

"The Little People?" the short man asked.

"It's what we call the puppets, sir, for indeed they do seem more than half alive sometimes." His voice hardened. "But since it seems there is someone here bound we'll not succeed with them, we'll likely *have* to move on, no matter what the doctor says."

68

"But you'd be willing to stay if you could?" the taller man asked.

"Most willing and glad. But a person must eat." Barney tried again to smile.

"Then it may be we can help. I, sir, am Lewis Hallam, manager of a Company of Comedians lately come from London, and this is my principal actor, Mr. Rigby."

"It is a pleasure to make your acquaintances, sirs."

"Thank you, Mr. Hormsby. We can return your compliment for we have often heard of the greatest ropedancer of them all. I wish I might have seen you."

Barney managed his smile this time, though it was a wry one. "Indeed, I do wish it myself, sir."

"Yes. Well now perhaps we can be mutually helpful one to another. As we came along Mr. Rigby and I were discussing our own problems and worrying over them. On Friday we will show our first play at the Playhouse here, which I have newly put into most excellent repair. We were, we thought, fully ready, but last night one of my candle snuffers, the lads who tend the candles that they do not drip and spoil the fine clothes of the gentry, was hauled away by his father, who is, I am told, lately come here from the Colony of Massachusetts and thinks the theater smacks of sin and the devil. We have not yet found another boy to fill his place and if you, Master Puppeteer," —he turned to Rom—"would like to have it, the place is yours."

Rom's face was a picture of confusions. Here was a job that would probably tide them over at least until Barney was fit again. He wanted to say yes to it, knew he must say yes. And yet, suppose his real father *were* of this Company as Polly had suggested! He said, "Oh, sir, I . . ." but Lewis Hallam interrupted him.

"Hear me out, young sir, before you answer. The work is none so full of magic but dull and drab for the most part. You'll be general errand boy as well as candle snuffer, and ordered about by my Company and cursed by the gallery. The pay will be small, though likely as much as you'd earn from your Little People. But you may now and again have a chance to walk upon the stage, though no speaking parts, mind you. Now, what say you?"

Rom looked at Barney, and Lewis Hallam, seeing the look, said, "Perhaps you'd like to withdraw a bit and talk of it with your father. If . . ."

"No need for that, Mr. Hallam," Barney said quickly, wondering what had got into Rom. "He'll come and gladly, and we thank you from our hearts for your kindness."

"It's no kindness," Hallam said. "As I said, we were at our wits' end to find a boy to suit us by the morrow." He turned to Rom. "Come tomorrow to the Playhouse, Master Puppeteer, and"—he glanced at Polly—"bring your sister with you. If she can sew a bit, and I don't doubt she can, we may find a place for her as well. Mistress Adcock, who cares for our wardrobe, was complaining but yesterday that she needed more help to keep the costumes in proper order."

"They'll both be there then, Mr. Hallam," Barney said, holding out his hand, "and once again we thank you."

CHAPTER SEVEN

Rom was up at daybreak next morning, bringing water from the well so they could scrub themselves to shining for their visit to the Playhouse. He had not slept much during the night. He had twisted and turned in his bunk bed, now pushing his thoughts ahead in eagerness to a real job with regular pay, now holding them back, fearing he would have to meet the man he hated.

He had told Barney his dread of coming face to face with Patrick Malone and had begged Barney to let him go to Mr. Hallam and take back his promise to be a candle snuffer. Barney thought he should, at least, wait before he gave up the opportunity. Barney said it wasn't likely Malone would be part of this Company. And if, by chance, he should be, there was no need for Rom to own him father. None but the three of them knew of the relationship, and it didn't stand to reason that a mere candle snuffer would see much of the actors. If the worst came and he did find Malone there, then he could leave the work just as soon as Mr. Hallam could replace him.

With that Rom had had to be content, but he was still worrying his problem when the rising sun crossed his face and he got up and woke Polly and went to fetch water for their washing. And he was silent and heavy-hearted as later he walked beside his sparkling, excited sister to their appointment.

They went through the town just shaking itself out for the day's work and came to the Capitol building. Polly had had no opportunity to look at it carefully and she stopped and stared at its two rounded brick wings joined by an areaway with graceful arched openings. "Why is it so, Rom?" she asked. "Why are there two buildings joined together?"

Rom had wondered about this himself and had asked the miller. He told her now what the miller had told him. "Because the two parts of the government meet and work in the two wings. One is for the House of Burgesses, who are chosen by the people of the Colony to represent them and who come from all over the place. The other is for the gentlemen of the General Court and the Governor's Council. Ben Post says each wing has its staircase within, and above yon arches is a great conference room where burgesses and councilors meet together for morning prayers and hold joint conferences when they cannot separately agree upon the good for the Colony."

"Could we go in and look at it?"

"Likely." Rom spoke shortly, wanting to get to the Playhouse and find out about Patrick Malone. "But not now. Come along, Pol, and hurry or we'll be late."

They went around the Capitol in its green square that sloped on the north side steeply down to the neat brick jail and the jail keeper's house. There were fewer buildings in the area east of the Capitol, and they could see the Theater standing stark and clear, almost touching the edge of the thick forest that stretched beyond it.

From the outside the Playhouse looked like nothing more than a long, red, wooden barn, roofed with iron and set sideways to face the road. The miller had told Rom it was the second theater to be built in Williamsburg. The first had not prospered and had long ago ceased to be used for its proper purpose. This new building was but a few years old. It had welcomed one company of players for two seasons, but they had made no plans for returning and the place had stood dark and dreaming, waiting for Lewis Hallam and his Company of Comedians.

As they came to the open door, Rom could count his own heavy heartbeats. There was no one near it and he hesitated a moment, then went in boldly with Polly at his heels. They entered a kind of narrow anteroom that stretched across the front of the building, which Rom guessed to be more than eighty feet long and a good thirty-six across. A door leading off from the anteroom was closed, and he wondered whether they should go through it or wait for someone to come for them.

"Why don't you shout?" Polly asked and giggled fool-ishly from nervousness.

"Well and I will," Rom said and raised his voice and called, "Hola! Is anyone here?"

Immediately the closed door opened and a man's head was stuck through. "Well?" he said, "what is it, boy, what is it? Must you make all that racket?"

Rom said, with dignity, "I do crave your pardon, sir. We are Romulus and Polly Hormsby and we were told to come here to . . ."

"Oh! The new Snuffles and the lass that's going to help Mistress Adcock. Why didn't you say so right off? Come in, come in then. Someone's sure to be about. Rigby! Ad-cock!"

He let the door close with a bang and left Rom and Polly to find their own way after him. They came into an empty theater, for the man had disappeared as if he had vanished into the air. Light slanted downwards in bands from three windows set high under the roof, hardly dis-turbing the general gloom of the place. For a moment they could see nothing, then, their eyes adjusting to the dimness, details began to come up clearly.

They were standing in a long, narrow room. In front of them were rows of backless benches covered with green baize and placed very close together. A gallery, also filled

74

with benches, rose steeply at one end of the room, and below it and along each side, railed boxes were draped in red velvet. The pit, the gallery, and the boxes, Rom thought, remembering tales he'd heard of English theaters, and felt a curious drumming in his head as excitement mounted in him.

He turned in the opposite direction and saw a platform raised some five feet from the floor and extending out into the pit. A sunken enclosure below it was, he guessed, for the musicians when they were needed. A row of iron spikes ran across the front of the stage and slanted inward toward a recessed trough. A green cloth curtain hung, somewhat askew, before an arched opening about eighteen feet above the spikes. He looked up and read, over the stage, the words

TOTUS MUNDUS AGIT HISTRIONEM

Beside him, Polly pointed to the words and whispered, "What does it say, Rom?"

Rom said slowly, trying to remember how to translate the Latin words accurately, "It means, I think, the whole world acts the player. And why are you whispering, Polly? We're not in church." He was wishing someone would come and tell them what to do, and he sounded irritated.

"In truth I don't know, Rom," Polly said. "I'm sorry, I . . ."

"Ho, there! Are you the two I'm supposed to show the ropes to?"

The voice came muffled from behind the green curtain. "Hold on but one little minute till I get this blasted thing up."

There was a creaking and groaning and the green curtain rose slowly until there was an opening in the arch some four feet high. There the curtain stuck and refused to budge, though they could hear the person who had called them pulling and jerking and addressing the curtain as if it were a live thing. Finally he gave up and stepped beneath the bottom edge and came out onto the forestage. He was a short, cheerful looking man, puffing a little from his struggle with the ropes.

"Blast the thing," he said, coming down to the edge of the stage. "It's always like this on day before opening. No matter how hard we try something's sure to get scrimped and have to be done over again. But all will be smooth by tomorrow night. Somehow the miracle always happens. Come along up, you two. No, wait! I'd best come down to you."

He disappeared again beneath the curtain and they watched his legs in neat brown stockings move quickly across the stage. A minute later they saw him on a flight of steps, dark-painted, along the wall to their right. "Now," he said, speaking very rapidly as he jumped from the steps to the pit, "a good morning to you both. I'm Jack Adcock, the least of all the players, though I'm handy with a song, if I do say it as shouldn't, and more than earn my share with sad songs and glad songs and funny songs and mad songs till they do be running from my ears. Welcome to the Company, Mistress Polly and Rom Hormsby. You'll find us a bit at sixes and sevens today, which we beg you overlook."

He stopped, out of breath, and rolled his eyes in pretended despair. Neither Rom nor Polly could think of anything to say, so they held their tongues and waited.

"Well, enough of that. And now to work. If you're ready, that is."

Rom said, "Whenever you are, sir," and thought they'd been ready for hours and hours, or so it seemed, but he doubted it became a candle snuffer to say so to an actor.

"We'll start where we are, then, and I'll show you what you'll have to do, Rom. Then we'll see the rest. It's a tight little theater. Better than some I've played in England, I can tell you. Old Hallam's done us proud. Where are those boys?"

He cupped his hands and shouted in the general direction of the stage, "Lewis! Adam! Where are you?"

An answer came, in a thin, small voice, from above their heads. "We're up here, Jack, among the ropes and things with Snuffles."

"Then stay there till I come, Adam. And do you and young Lewis try to keep out of mischief. . . . Not that they will with Snuffles about," he added to himself. "Come along now."

He walked over to the long wall of the Theater. Polly and Rom followed and watched as he explained Rom's work.

"Ever been in a playhouse before, Snuffles?"

"No, sir, and my name is Romulus, sir, or Rom."

Adcock raised an eyebrow at him and said in a tight sort of voice, "Is it so? You'd best get used to Snuffles or Johnnie from now on, for that's what you'll answer to, be you Rom or the Angel Gabriel."

"Why, sir?" Polly put in hurriedly, seeing the danger signals in Rom's cheeks.

"Don't know, mistress." Adcock was friendly again. "That's the way it is in the theater. Always has been and always will be. Custom. Tradition." He put his hand on Rom's shoulder and gave it a small squeeze and Rom's anger went away. He guessed Mr. Adcock meant only to be kind and give him a chance to become accustomed to the new and, somehow, insulting name.

"Well now, Snuffles, do you see yon rows of candle holders upon the walls?"

"Yes, sir."

"You'll wait each night close to them and keep your ears open and your feet ready to run. When you hear the call, "*Snuffles!*" do you go to the light nearest the sound and put a fresh candle in the sconce, else there'll be a riot, for candles when they burn low do drip hot wax no matter what we do and there's like to be trouble if the fresh one's not put in and that in a hurry. Understood?"

77

Rom nodded. "Do I watch all the candles?"

"No. There'll be two of you, one to each side. In a bit we'll fetch some candles and you can practice making the change quickly and quietly. And you'd best find time before tomorrow night to learn where each holder is and the quickest way to get to it."

"That I will," Rom promised.

"Is that all he has to do, sir?" Polly asked.

"Not by a long chance," Adcock said, laughing a little, "though once the play begins it'll be enough. Other times he'll be fetching and carrying and doing the bidding of every actor in the Company from Old Hallam to young Lewis, who fancies himself an actor though he's not yet crossed a stage."

Rom sighed, and wondered when, if ever, he'd find time to explore this new and tempting world he'd felt opening to him so short a time before. Adcock said, "Do not lose heart, Snuffles. It's not so bad a life if you can but come to love the stage a bit."

"I could do so," Rom said, and Adcock said, "Good. Then you'll not mind the work, Snuffles, for you'll see more of the theater behind the stage in a season than you'd ever see in a lifetime from the pit. Now, come along and we'll have a look at the rest of the place. You'll likely have to wait to meet the Company for no one's about save me and the Hallam boys, though Mrs. Adcock will be in before you leave to talk to Mistress Polly."

He took them up onto the stage and showed them the grooves in the floor in which painted scenes of streets and forests and rooms slid from each side of the stage. He pointed out five great hoops each holding twelve candles and the trough behind the spikes which, at play time, was filled with lighted wicks floating in oil to give more light to the actors. Polly asked the reason for the iron spikes and he said they were to keep the audience from swarming upon the stage in order to censure or praise the play.

"Look up," he said to them. "That's the very heart and center of our stage. We'll go aloft in a bit and I'll show you

78

the thunder machine and the ropes and pulleys that control the curtain and the flying contraption."

"Flying contraption?" Polly asked.

"See there above you?" He pointed to a kind of chair on ropes, swinging idly in the dark, shadowed space above them. "It's used when we need to bring a god down from heaven or send a man up to it. We call it the god's chair."

He led them next to a steep ladder nailed against the wall, shouting as he went, "Hola, Adam! Young Lewis! We're coming up."

The ladder ended at a narrow plank walkway that threaded, high above the stage, through a maze of beams and ropes and pulleys that made up the sinews of this world of make-believe.

"Jack!" The voice was the same they had heard before and it was followed at once by a small figure coming at great speed along the plank walk. "Where have you been, Jack?"

"You know where I've been, Adam." Adcock was in front of Rom and Polly, and they could not see the boy he talked to. "Showing the new Snuffles and his sister the Theater, as your father commanded."

"Oh. I had forgot. Where is he, then, the new Snuffles? Is he like the old one?"

"See for yourself, Adam. Come along past me, Mistress Polly and Snuffles, and meet the youngest person in our Company."

Adcock squeezed himself against the wall to let Polly by, and when she flattened herself beside him, Rom inched his way ahead of them both and stood before the boy. Adam Hallam was, he guessed, ten years old but his face looked much younger. It was dull and childish and held a perpetually frightened look. He stared at Rom from lackluster eyes whose irises showed a pale, china blue in his white, thin face. He did not speak, and Rom was about to greet him kindly, for he felt sorry for the child, when another boy older by some two years, came along the walk and stopped and looked Rom up and down and said, "So!

79

You're the new Snuffles! Well, you'd best look sharp when I call or I'll tell my father and he'll be rid of you quickly."

"Mind your tongue, young Lewis, and remember that manners maketh the man." Adcock spoke sharply from the shadows. "Do you pay proper attention to your own behavior and leave Rom Hormsby to his. Just being your father's son gives you no right to be rude."

"Oh," Lewis said grumpily, "I didn't see you in the shades, Jack."

"I guessed as much," Adcock said dryly. "Now do you and Adam go along back and let us finish here, for I've other work to do. And see you behave yourselves."

Young Lewis turned and started back along the walk. Even his back looked sullen, Rom thought, hoping he'd not have much to do with the conceited young donkey. He felt even sorrier for the younger brother, who was likely always around to be bullied, and remembering he had in his pocket a packet of sweetmeats Mistress Struthers had given him, he said, "Here, Adam, we'll be friends, won't we?" and handed the child a piece of the sticky sweet and saw his eyes grow big with surprise and pleasure as he popped it into his mouth and chewed it solemnly. "Now get along with you, young one, as Mr. Adcock says."

Adam turned himself about in the narrow space and took one step away and stopped and came back again and put his hand into Rom's and said softly, "I like you, Snuffles. You're not like the other, because he's mean. I'll call *you* Johnnie." He was gone then, running along the walk as if it were the wide, solid floor of the forest. Rom called after him, "Do you call me Rom, Adam, for it's my name," and heard the child's high laughter answer him.

He turned back to speak to Polly about the child and saw her face white and frightened. She was swaying toward the edge of the walk, and he took a great step and reached her and grabbed her about the waist, drawing her back from the edge and steadying her.

"What is it, Polly? Are you ill?" he asked, and Ad-

80

cock said, "What happened? What's amiss with Mistress Polly?"

Polly drew in her breath sharply and shuddered and hid her face in Rom's shoulder.

"Easy, Pol," he said, "easy, girl. You are safe enough now. I'll not let you fall."

She lifted her face and tried to smile, but her eyes held the remembrance of fear and Rom said again, "What is it, Polly? You're afeared and that's not like you. What frightened you?"

"There," Polly said, pointing, "the—the god's chair."

Adcock said, "What about it, mistress?"

"There is—there was—a great hairy—hairy beast in it. Just now. For one moment. When you were talking to Adam, Rom."

Adcock started to laugh, thinking the girl was having a jape at their expense, and saw her face clearly and knew she was really afraid and shouted, "Young Lewis! Lewis Hallam! Do you come back here this instant!" He added gently to Polly, "Do not fear, lass. There was no great beast, you can be sure. We'll find out what you did see. *Lewis!*"

"Do you want me, Jack?"

Young Lewis Hallam appeared, it seemed, from nowhere, and Rom felt Polly shaking again and could have slapped the smirking face beside him.

"I do, young Lewis. And I'll thank you next time I call to come properly along the walk instead of dropping from the beams to scare the wits from the young lady who's already had one bad fright."

"Very well, Jack. I did not mean to make anyone, least of all a lady, afeared," Lewis said in so mild and sorrowful a voice Rom would have believed him had he not seen his eyes, which were cruel and mocking.

"I'd not lay a wager you didn't, you young devil," Adcock said. "Now what were you doing in the god's chair?"

"Me, Jack? I've not been near the god's chair this day."

"Who has been then?"

"Indeed I could not say, Jack, save it were Adam."

"You know right well Adam hates the thing and fears it. Where's Snuffles?"

"Why there before you, Jack."

"None of your insolence, young Lewis. You well know I mean the other Snuffles."

82

"How should I know where he is, Jack? Why?"

"Now hark you, young Lewis. Mistress Polly did but now see what looked to be a great beast in the chair and she near fell from the walk for fear and I'd not blame her. I'll warrant you know something of it and I'm bound you'll tell me."

Lewis laughed. "Are you, Jack?" he said softly. "I've seen no beast about."

"Now, young Lewis," Adcock said patiently, "we know there was no beast. I know it. Snuffles here knows it. Mistress Polly knows it. And, of course, you know it. But something—or more likely, somebody—was there and deliberately frightened her. Someone's been at the costumes, as is plain, young Lewis. I say it was you."

"I doubt you could prove it, Jack Adcock," Lewis said, and smiled a nasty smile. Rom wanted to hit him with his fists. He recognized the thought with surprise, knowing it was the first time he'd ever wanted such a thing, but he had no time to think about it further.

"Likely not, young Lewis," Adcock was saying, "but I can tell your father and then we'll see if a birching will loosen your tongue."

Young Lewis said evenly, "Try it, Jack Adcock. My . . ." but Polly interrupted him. She thought she could not stand here upon the narrow walk another moment. What was done was done and all she wanted was to be away from this high, cluttered place and safe on firm ground below. Then she could start forgetting the thing she'd seen. "Perhaps Lewis is right, Mr. Adcock," she said quickly. "Likely I did but see a great shadow yonder and imagined it a beast. The light is none too good. Pray, let us talk no more of it."

Adcock looked at her closely. Poor lass. Likely she wants only to be out of here, he thought. And who was to blame her. Besides he knew young Lewis. The boy was a great bully, puffed up with pride in being the manager's son and spoiled as well. No matter what he was told, Old Hallam would never take the rod to young Lewis and young Lewis knew it, more's the pity. Adcock lifted his hands and dropped them and said, "As you wish, mistress. Let us go down then."

CHAPTER EIGHT

The sun was nearly noon high when Rom went next day to the Playhouse to discover the quickest and quietest way to each candle in the house. Polly had gone earlier to Daniel Fisher's tenement where Mr. Hallam and his company were housed.

She had met Mistress Adcock yesterday when they had, at last, come down from the heights above the stage, and had taken at once to the gentle, middle-aged woman who served the company as both actress and wardrobe mistress. Mistress Adcock had questioned Polly about her skill at needlework and, satisfied by the answers, had welcomed her warmly as a needed assistant and bade her come early next morning to begin her work.

Rom had spent the morning with the Little People, checking the rods that controlled the movements of their arms and legs and heads, airing their costumes, and smoothing and folding the miniature clothes and putting them away in the leather box, pondering while he worked the fright that might have sent Polly to death.

She had told him, once they were away from the Playhouse, there *had* surely been something big and hairy in that chair, something with a beast's face and a beast's great paws. She was sure she had not imagined it, and it did not occur to Rom to doubt her. He had remembered Mr. Adcock's question to Lewis about the costumes and guessed someone had dressed himself in a beast's clothes and hidden to frighten the newcomers as a jape. He had told Polly his guess and she had agreed it must have been so, but it could have been a dangerous jape if Rom had not been there to catch her, she said. "It couldn't have been Lewis, then," she had added, "for he came too quickly in his ordinary clothes when Mr. Adcock called. Besides, whoever it was in the beast costume must have been bigger and broader than Lewis."

"Well, I'll warrant Lewis knew all about it. Do you keep as far as possible away from him, Polly. I don't like his face and I'm sure he bullies Adam."

Now as he rounded the Capitol to the Theater he was wondering who could have done such a cruel and stupid thing. He thought if he could in any way discover the answer he would take the story to Mr. Hallam, and at once he felt ashamed that he should think of such talebearing rather than of punishing the joker with his own fists. He thought it would do little good to bear the tale in any case, for he could not do so with proof and he doubted Mr. Hallam would hear him otherwise. He sighed and lifted his shoulders and went into the empty Theater and spent the next hour or two learning how to get from any spot in the house to any other with speed and quiet.

He did not see Polly or indeed any of the Company. He guessed they were all in their own places preparing for the opening tonight, and when he was satisfied he had done all he could he left the Theater and wandered into the forest, thinking to find a quiet place to eat the bread and cheese and the apple he had this morning put in his pocket.

He had only walked a short distance when he saw, ahead of him, a deer standing stock-still in the open space between two tall, thick holly trees already showing a blush of winter red in their berries. Rom stopped, and for a second or two he and the deer looked at one another curiously before the creature, taking flight, bounded off to the right and broke through a thicket of myrtleberry bushes. Rom ran after her, hoping to see once more the graceful movement as she leaped in the shining air.

She had gone by the time he had followed her through the gap in the myrtleberry. He should have known he could not hope to catch her. He stood still, feeling his nostrils tickled by the clean, spicy smell of the tiny wax-coated new leaves she had bruised in her passing, looking about him with delight and wonder.

He was in a forest room. Dark conifers arched above him, their branches meeting and interlocking to form a ceiling in which bits of sunlight and brilliant sky seemed trapped and held for his delight. The ground beneath his feet was soft and fragrant with needles dropped no one could say how many ages before. The whole space was cut off from the rest of the forest by the myrtleberry thicket. In one corner, opposite the place where he had entered behind the doe, someone had once built a rude kind of shelter of wattles woven and caulked with clay. It looked from where he stood surprisingly sound and he guessed the tree ceiling had kept out the worst of the weather and so preserved the small hut. He walked across the springy floor and came to it and saw it was fitted with a rough plank door which had once been held by leather straps now partly rotted away. The door swung crazily, half-open, but Rom thought it could be made tight again with a pair of iron hinges and a lock. He looked through the opening and could see nothing but gloom and found a pine knot oozing resin and lighted it with his tinderbox and held it high. The interior of the little house was clean and sweet-smelling. At its back wall a spring of clear water, evidently fed by an underground stream, bubbled and gurgled before it trickled away beneath the wall.

Rom was enchanted. Here was a place he could call his own. If it had ever belonged to anybody, he doubted if it did any longer. He would take it over and fit a proper door to it and a lock and he would keep it secret as a refuge place for himself. Maybe, later, he would tell Polly of it— if he felt like it. But, for now, he would not tell anybody.

The pine knot sputtered and Rom went back into the day and carefully put out what was left of the light and remembered he was hungry and sat down with his back to one of the pine boles. He ate his bread and cheese and the sharp, sweet apple and forgot his problems and was content as he had not been since he left England. When he had finished his lunch he scattered the crumbs upon the pine needles for some hungry bird and folded the napkin that had held his food and started back to the Playhouse, singing one of the songs that Shakespeare had written, to a tune he had learned from a wandering song-ster at a fair:

> "Under the greenwood tree
> Who loves to lie with me,
> And turn his merry note
> Unto the sweet bird's throat,
> Come hither, come hither, come hither:
> Here shall he see
> No enemy
> But winter and rough weather."

He was still singing when he entered the Playhouse. He had spent more time than he had thought in his new-found sanctuary and it was nearing six o'clock, when the play was to begin. As he opened the door into the pit he could sense the bustle and hurry going on behind the lowered curtain and below the stairs that led to the dressing rooms. Across the floor of the pit he saw a shadow figure lighting the candles in their sconces on the far side of the house. That must be the other Snuffles. He thought the figure was familiar, but he had no time to wonder why for he was already late to his duties and that on his first night. What would Mr. Hallam think if he knew?

He hurried to the corner of the stage, thankful he had already put beside the musicians' place the candles he would need later, and the long taper for lighting them. He lit the taper and, from it, the candle nearest him and the next and the next, moving quickly around the wall toward the stairway that led up to the gallery. As he came to the point where he could step into the nearest box he paused and looked across to the other side, and nearly dropped the taper.

Black Rafe Bascomb was exactly opposite him, holding a taper like his, staring at him with an evil, sneering smile. Black Rafe was the other Snuffles!

Rom was paralyzed. He thought he could not move if he were to be hung for it. He remembered how Adam had said yesterday, "Snuffles is with us," and he knew as if he'd seen him that Black Rafe had worn the beast's costume to frighten Polly.

What could he do now? He was fair caught. He was at Black Rafe's mercy. He felt the trembling start in his legs, felt the fear knots in his stomach. He wondered if there were a chance of somebody—anybody—coming to his rescue. He wondered whether he could yell, call out for help, and doubted he would so shame himself even if it would do any good.

"Do you not be afeared, little mannikin," Black Rafe called softly, almost pleasantly, across the space between them. "Black Rafe will no hurt you." The voice went cold and hard and menacing. "Not yet. Your time has not come

89

for punishment. But it will. Do you not think I have forgot the day in my lane."

The trembling left Rom's legs. The knots in his stomach relaxed. He took a firmer hold on the taper and jumped into the box. Somehow he knew Black Rafe meant what he said. Somehow he knew he was, for now, safe. What would happen later . . .

He had no time to worry about that. Already the first of the playgoers were coming into the gallery: prentices and servants, giggling and shoving each other good humoredly. Rom ran softly through the boxes lighting the last candle just as the head of the first of the box-seat holders appeared at the top of the stairs leading from the stage door.

Somewhere behind the curtain a trumpet sounded. The tall graceful man who had been with Mr. Hallam at the Market Square moved in from the wings to the center of the stage just behind the footlight trough and began to address the audience in the customary prologue. Rom, at first, heard little of it, for his ears were turned outward in fear lest he should lose the first cry of *"Snuffles!"* Gradually he began to realize the candles would not burn down for a bit and he gave part of his attention to the stage. The actor, (What had Mr. Hallam named him? Rigby? Yes, Rigby.) was coming to the end of the long verses he had been repeating.

"For us, then, and our Muse, thus low I bend,"

the light, pleasant voice was saying,

"Nor fear to find in each the warmest friend;
Each smiling aspect dissipates our fear
We ne'er can fail of kind protection here;
The stage is ever wisdom's favorite care:
Accept our labors, then, approve our pains
Your smiles will please us equal to our gains
And as you all esteem the Darling Muse
The gen'rous plaudit you will not refuse."

90

He swept off his hat and made a deep and graceful bow and withdrew again into the wings while the audience, obviously pleased, clapped their hands and whistled their approval. Then the green curtain began slowly and smoothly and quietly to rise, as Mr. Adcock had promised it would, and three men, handsomely dressed in the style of the day, walked out upon the stage closing behind them the scene painted to represent a street in Venice.

"In sooth, I know not why I am so sad:
It wearies me; you say it wearies you;
But how I caught it, found it, or came by it,
What stuff 'tis made of, whereof it is born,
I am to learn;
And such a want-wit sadness makes of me
That I have much ado to know myself."

The opening lines of *The Merchant of Venice* were as familiar to Rom as his prayers, but they held him in a new kind of thralldom. The men and women posturing on the stage; the rich, brilliant costumes; the candles flaring in their hoops and the lighted wicks floating in the foot trough; the smell of candle wax; the fine ladies whispering in the boxes; and the prentices shuffling in the gallery, made of Shakespeare's sweet words something new and different; living and exciting and moving, a thing beyond a dream.

Halfway through the second act came the first shouted *"Snuffles."* Rom heard it and hated it because it pulled him away from the stage, but he ran to replace the guttering candle with a fresh one before the hot wax had time to damage the man seated beneath it.

The scene had changed to a room in a house, when he could return to his watching. Two ladies were on the stage. Standing in the wings, where Rom from his place at one side of the stage could see him, young Lewis Hallam was preparing to make his first entrance as an actor. He was clearly nervous. He fussed with his costume and shifted his feet and kept twisting his head from side to side as if he looked for a way of escape. Rom thought, remembering the scene to come, Lewis had little cause for fright. He was playing a servant to Portia and had only to come on the stage, speak one line, and go off again. Any fool, even fearful Adam, could do it, Rom thought.

The moment for Lewis's entrance came. Someone gave him a little push and he all but fell onto the stage. For a full minute, he stood there, staring at the audience, his knees visibly shaking, saying no word of his line. Then he burst into tears and fled, leaving the other actors to get on with the scene as best they could.

Rom grinned to himself. Served him right, the spoiled boaster. Maybe he'd be less quick to jeer at other people after this.

"*Snuffles!*"

Another candle going, Rom thought. He would be glad to get back to the caravan and his bed this night. His legs felt as if they were ready to break off at the knees. No doubt he'd get used to it in time. Meantime, he ran.

But he forgot to think about his tiredness when *The Merchant of Venice* and another, shorter play called *The Anatomist* were over and the curtain fell on the first production offered in Williamsburg by the Hallam Company of Comedians. When the audience had left the Playhouse, chattering and laughing and very obviously pleased, and Rom was snuffing the last candle, Mr. Adcock came to the middle of the steps that led beneath the stage and called, "Hist! Rom! Come along. Old Hallam says you and Mistress Polly are to join the Company in the greenroom. She's there already with my wife, so do you hurry."

They were all there, or seemed to be, actors and actresses; some still costumed, their faces powdered and painted for their parts; others in their regular clothes. They were laughing and talking in shrill, happy voices, sure they would have a good season here in Williamsburg. They were gathered about Mr. Hallam, and Mr. Adcock said they were waiting for the share-out which took place after each performance.

"Share-out?" Rom asked.

"It is thus we are paid our wages as actors. You see, Rom, we are a—a stock company and each player has a share in the whole. In our Company there are eighteen shares, four for paying the costs, which include your due and Mistress Polly's. Those four are called the Company Share. Old Hallam has two shares since he is both actor and manager. And that leaves one share each for the eleven other actors, including the young Hallams, for even Adam, though he does not act as yet, is counted a member of the Company."

Rom scarcely heard him. He had seen Rafe leaning against the far wall watching him, and he was feeling half ill. He heard Polly calling, "Rom! Rom!" and he forced himself to look away from Rafe and go to her.

"Quiet! Quiet! The Company."

Old Hallam was standing beside a table covered with a green cloth. He held a leather bag that looked heavy. The laughter and talk ceased and the company crowded about him. "It's been a good night," Hallam said, "Pray our Goddess they will all be so in Williamsburg."

Someone shouted "Say amen to that!" and everyone laughed again.

Hallam opened the bag and carefully poured into a heap on the table the pile of coins it contained. The candle flame winked on silver and gold pieces as he divided the coins, quickly, for he was long accustomed to this sorting, into eighteen piles. He pushed four of them together and to one side, put two of the remainder in his own pocket, and began to call the names of the Company.

He began with Polly who came up and was given her wage for the day from the Company Share. Black Rafe's name came next. He sidled to the table, snatched his coins from Hallam, and sidled off again without a word. Then Rom heard his own name and took the money

handed to him and said, "My thanks, Mr. Hallam, for your
kindness to me and my sister."

Hallam looked a little startled, as if he had not expected
to be thanked. "No play on the morrow, Snuffles," he said
to Rom, "but you'd better put in an appearance in case
you're needed here." He called Rigby's name then and the
share-out went on, while Rom and Polly watched. When

there was but one pile left Hallam said, "Patrick" and Rom's breath caught. "Patrick Malone! Where is the . . ."

The room swam about Rom and his knees seemed to be buckling under him. He had given no single thought during the busy moments of this exciting day to the thing that had nagged his mind persistently this month past. And here it was—what he had been dreading and hoping for with a wild hope born of anger and hate. Here it was and he was so blinded by his own emotion he could not even see the face he was prepared to loathe on sight.

He felt an arm thrust through his and heard Polly speaking softly at his side. "Have a care, Rom. This is not the place to make a scene."

"Cease your bellowing, Lewis. Here I am and I doubt yon money will grow feet and walk away while it awaits my pocket."

The voice was warm and deep and full of laughter.

Rom's eyes focused and he found he could see clearly the room and the people in it and Polly holding his arm tight and looking sorely troubled as if she were afeared of what he might do. He looked steadily where the others were looking and saw an elderly man, of no great height, with a ruddy face and eyes that matched the laughter in his voice. He was wearing still the black loose robe he had worn in the play and Rom realized this was the man whose acting had charmed him in the part of Shylock. It came to Rom with a feeling of shock that he did not look a villain, this Patrick Malone. His whole face spoke of kindness and love of living and of his fellow creatures. He was merry and free of care and radiated good fellowship. How could he be the one who had ordered his own children abandoned? And yet . . .

Lines from another of Shakespeare's plays came into Rom's head as if someone were whispering them to him:

> O villain, villain, smiling, damned villain!
> My tables,—meet it is I set it down,
> That one may smile, and smile, and be a villain.

95

So Hamlet had been right. This smiling, gracious man—his father, his own father—was yet, in truth, a villain. He started forward, forgetting where he was, and felt himself held strongly back and heard Polly saying over and over again, "No, Rom! No. No. No. Not now. Not here. No, Rom! No!"

She's right, he thought. He wanted no one to interfere between himself and his father. He would wait until they two could be alone, but he would not wait long. There, the Company was already leaving the greenroom, following Old Hallam who had waved and gone quickly once Patrick Malone had claimed his share.

Rom wrenched his arm away from Polly and when she would have stayed him further or gone with him, whispered to her, "Leave me alone, Polly. What I must do, I must do by myself," so fiercely she moved from him and for a moment he stood alone in the room and the world and knew it and felt the desolation of loneliness in his mind and heart. Then he almost ran across the room to the door through which the loose, black robe was disappearing.

The corridor was dark and empty except for the two of them. The black robe was a darker shadow in the gloom lit only by one candle at each end of the passage. I'll lose him, Rom thought, and called out harshly, "Malone! Patrick Malone!"

The black figure stopped and turned, "Who is it in the press who calls on me?" Malone said, and Rom, beneath the roiling of his mind, marked the words as a quotation from Shakespeare's play about Julius Caesar. Malone peered along the corridor toward him, squinting a little. "Ah, so," he said. "It's the new Snuffles, isn't it? What can I do for you then, lad?"

Rom had come up to him and stood before him, face red and puffed in anger, feet spread wide apart, hands balled into fists at his side. "This, you—you—smiling, damned villain, you unnatural father, you—you . . ." He spluttered, choking and the more angry therefore. Patrick Malone was *laughing* at him.

Rom raised his hand to strike the actor.

Malone, seeing the gesture begin, still laughing a little through his bewilderment, caught the hand in mid-air and held it there in so strong a grip Rom winced with the pain of it. "You should not strike a man before you tell him the cause of your anger," Malone said in perfect good humor. "That's not the part of a gentleman and, Snuffles though you be, you have about you the look of breeding." He dropped Rom's hand and heard the half sob of relief from the pain and added, "Your pardon for hurting you. I'd no mind to feel yon fist in my face. No, not though you insult me with lines from the great Shakespeare himself. Now what, and it please you, is your quarrel with me?"

Rom clenched his jaws to stop the chattering of his teeth. It seemed an added injury, somehow, that Malone could quote Shakespeare's lines as easily and aptly as he could himself. He spoke tightly. "Do you pretend you do not know? Look at me."

Malone shook his head. "There's no pretending. In truth I do not know what angers you or what you hold against me. And, do I look never so hard, I see nothing but an angry face."

"Do you deny—do you dare deny that ten years ago you caused your son and daughter to be abandoned and left, for all of you, to die? Do you dare deny that?"

"Certainly I dare and I call on the God of Hosts to witness it, sir. Who has been telling you such witch tales I do not know. Do *you* hear *me* now. I am Patrick Malone, actor, a lone man always. I am not nor have I ever been married. Nor have I sired any children throughout a long and no doubt often misspent life and the more's the pity of it entirely. And this—all of it—you can prove upon me by any of the Company but most especially by Old Lewis Hallam himself and his good wife who have known me well since we were all young ones."

The pent-up anger and hatred left Rom in a long, sobbing gasp. He was empty and exhausted and weak. He covered his face with his arm and swayed a little and would have fallen had not Patrick Malone caught and held him gently. "Oh, sir—oh—sir," he said, and Malone hushed him and soothed him as if he had been a babe. "There, lad, there. No harm's done. Do you come with me and we'll find the bottom of this mystery before another hour's spent."

CHAPTER NINE

The cool mid-September night sparkled with stars as Rom ran back to the caravan. He wondered how he could ever have felt tired. The hour with Patrick Malone in his dressing room beneath the stage, telling him the story of the two deserted children and the misunderstood benefit ticket in their box, had lifted his heart and given him a deeper rest than he had known for a long time. For Malone had not badgered him with doubts about the meaning of the letter. He had nodded and clucked his tongue and believed, or seemed to believe, every word Rom said. Best of all, Malone had understood his feeling of loss because he was rootless, because he had no name and so no identity of his own. Malone had sighed, and put his arm about Rom in sympathy and said in his deep, warm voice with the suggestion of Irish in it, "Aye, Romulus, it do be a hard thing to be nameless. Yet, do you not despair, for you will take your borrowed name, I'm thinking, and make it, in time, your own and such a fine and noble thing you'll be proud to bear it and pass it along to your children and your children's children. For it's not a name that makes the man but the man that makes a name."

Pat, for it was so he'd bade Rom call him, had tried to remember the ticket but could not. "Bring it along to me on the morrow, Rom. It may be sight of it will tease my memory. There've been so many years and so many plays and so many benefits it's hard to pick one from the air and say, 'That's it entirely!' But seeing the bit of paper may help my remembering and it may be I can call to mind something to help you know your right name."

Rom had promised, and they had left the Playhouse together and walked together as far as the Capitol and separated to go their different ways, each knowing in his heart he had found a friend.

The dark bulk of the mill showed ahead, its sails still for the wind had died to a sigh, and beyond it the humped shadow that was home. Rom slowed to a walking pace and began to sing softly to a tune of his own making the song of Autolycus from *The Winter's Tale:*

"Jog on, jog on, the foot-path way,
And merrily hent the stile-a:
A merry heart goes all the day,
Your sad tires in a mile-a."

The ending of the song brought him to the caravan. He could tell from the regular, deep snores coming through the door that Papa was asleep. On tiptoe, Rom crawled through the opening and began quietly to make himself ready for bed.

Polly heard his rustlings and got up and pulled on a dressing gown and looked through the cubbyhole curtain, half afraid of what she might see. Starshine came faintly through the door and showed her Rom, obviously in a fine and happy mood, and she could not still her curious mind. She slipped through the curtain and touched him on the arm and beckoned him into her sleeping place. He followed and sat beside her on the rumpled bed and told her all that had befallen.

When the telling was done he yawned and stretched and stood up, then bent to kiss her good night. She wanted to scold him for not coming at once to tell her what had happened, but all she said was, "Oh, Rom. I'm so glad it is so. I'm glad Patrick Malone is not our father. I—I *like* him."

"And so do I," Rom said, and added slowly, "but I'm not sure I'll take him the ticket tomorrow. It—it might jog his memory and bring to it something I'd rather not know."

Polly sighed. She thought he'd better know whatever there was to know or else be haunted by wondering the rest of his life, but she guessed this was no time to argue it out with him. "Wait till tomorrow before you decide. And best ask Papa. You *did* promise."

"Yes, but . . ."

"Get along now, Rom. It's late and we've both to be at work tomorrow. Let us sleep now."

He told the tale again next morning to Barney when their breakfast was over and Rom and Polly had gleefully added their first wages to the coins in the purse and rejoiced at the little added weight. Barney thought about the story a long time without saying anything. When he did speak he said only, "Well, Rom?"

"I don't think I'll take the ticket to Pat, Papa. I think it best not to try again, ever, to find our father. Because we might succeed and that would likely only stir again the anger and hating in my heart which is still now."

"There's that, Rom." Barney spoke slowly, not meeting Rom's look, and stopped. He's not done yet, Rom thought, and squirmed a little inside his clothes, sensing in Papa disappointment that he would so readily run from unpleasantness. He wondered what Papa would add, and waited, tightening his shoulders against whatever was to come. After all it was *his* unpleasantness, not Papa's nor even Polly's since she didn't seem to care.

"But hark you, Romulus." Barney still didn't look at him. "It's no use to run from yourself. Yon Patrick Malone has driven away that anger and hatred for a time and I say God bless him for that. But has he driven it off for all time, Rom? Or is it lying in you yet, deep hidden, sleeping maybe, but ready to spring out at you, screeching and screaming like a catamountain when you're least ready for it?"

Rom said, "Likely."

"Then you'd best keep on with your search. Best have a —a true mark for what's working inside you than risk it rotting and festering till it must needs break out at anything—or anybody, for the matter of that—because the evil's grown too great hiding in the dark and silence within your mind. Do you see what I'm meaning, Rom?"

Rom said nothing. He could not. He knew Papa was right, but he didn't want to admit it, didn't want to lose his new-found lightness of spirit or, indeed, to own himself wrong. He held his silence for a time and a time, while Barney watched him and he wrestled within himself. He knew he would have to give up in the end, knew he would have to agree with Papa, but he grudged the doing of it and when he did speak the words came without graciousness.

"Very well. I'll take the ticket. So much I will do. But I'll not promise to go beyond. I'll not promise to seek more news of my—my father."

"Well, that's enough for now, Rom. I'll fetch the ticket," Barney said, and made slow way to the corner, leaving his crutch behind, and opened his strong box and took out the mussed paper.

Polly had been watching Rom and paying little attention to Barney. As he made his way back with difficulty the hobbling sound of his coming reached out to her and she turned and saw his hard progress and said, scoldingly, "Papa! You should not be without your crutch. Stay right there while I fetch it to you."

"Do *you* stay, Polly," Barney said with the first easy grin he'd shown for weeks. "I'm doing without my crutch because yon Dr. Hay told me to do so."

"Papa!" she said, as he handed the ticket to Rom, "it's mending. Your leg is really mending."

"Better than that, Polly. It's mended! I went yesterday to the good doctor and he poked me and thumped me and banged me till I thought to have no leg left. And at the end he said I'd do. He said I'd come along faster than he'd dared hope and I'd best throw away yon crutch and learn to do without it. Next week, he said, when muscles have relearned their accustomed ease I'm to go and see his friend Mr. William Hunter at the Printing Office. Mr. Hunter has but recently lost a journeyman and will likely be glad enough to take on a master printer at journeyman's pay."

"Oh, Papa!" Polly hugged him and put her face on his shoulder to hide the tears in her eyes, happy tears though they were. Rom thumped him on the back, forgetting irritation, and even Betsy, hearing the commotion, stopped grazing and let out a long, low whinny.

"Now do you give over, Rom and Polly, and be off with you," Barney said, "or you'll be late to your work and I'll have no whit of breath left in my body."

Patrick Malone was already waiting at the Playhouse for Rom. No other person was about and the two sat on one of the hard benches in the pit while Patrick Malone turned the ticket about and about in his hands. He knew it well enough and his eyes misted with the remembering it brought.

"Ah, Rom," he said, "I was younger then. This was my first benefit. I had waited a long time for it and I was sorely puffed up in my pride. We were a traveling company and I but the least of them. But I could sing a bit in those days and I knew every song in *The Beggar's Opera* backwards and forwards and I was a sight lighter in the middle and slimmer in the leg than any of the other players. So, when the principal actor began coughing himself to death the manager ordered me to try the role of Macheath, and to everyone's surprise, not least my own, the people out front liked me. And so, when we came to Bath, I was granted a benefit of my own."

Patrick stopped speaking and he puckered up his eyebrows and shook his head a little while Rom thought about Bath, wondering what it was like there. Patrick flicked the ticket with his fingernail and stood up. "There's something else, Rom. Something that teases me sorely, a memory of something seen and seen again, something that relates in some manner to that very town but I cannot bring it back."

Rom held his breath, hoping Patrick would not bring the lost memory into focus, fearing to face again so soon his unwanted search. Suppose this memory found itself and tied itself to some other member of the Company. Old Hallam himself or Jack Adcock or Mr. Rigby. Rom couldn't bear the thought, not now, not when he was feeling peaceful and almost reconciled to his namelessness and almost as if he had found, in the Company, a place where he could belong. He pressed his hands together, watching the knuckles whiten, waiting for Patrick Malone to find his memory.

Patrick shook his head again in a bewildered way and handed the ticket back to Rom and said, "It's no use, Rom. The more I think the further away it goes."

Rom loosed his breath in a long sigh, and Patrick thought it a sigh of disappointment and tried to comfort him, "Do you not fret, Romulus. Keep the ticket and I'll think on it again, it may be with more success another time."

Rom thanked him and did not say how glad he was the memory hid itself still. For a little time at least he could hold to his peace.

The days moved in a glory of turning leaves toward full autumn and in time Rom stopped looking at Patrick Malone with an anxious questioning whenever they came together. For Patrick's memory stayed tight locked in his mind.

On the three nights each week when plays were given Rom stood to his candles and, between calls for fresh lights, watched the actors going about and about, threading their magic way among their many different parts in many different plays. The watching never staled for him, and each performance was a new miracle of make-believe made real and living before his eyes. He wished with all his heart and mind that he, too, could learn the craft of acting and stay here with this group of friendly people in the town he was coming to love and feel at home in, for the rest of his days.

Between performances he fetched and carried cheerfully enough, not grumbling that, more often than not, he did the chores of both snuffles, for Black Rafe slunk away as fast as he could when the candles were put out and shirked as much of his other work as he could. Polly was indignant and vowed she'd go herself and complain to Old Hallam if Rom would not. Rom hushed her. He didn't mind, he said. The more chance he had to be about the Theater, the better he liked it. He did not tell her his real reason for not minding. He did not say he feared Black Rafe Bascomb and was glad of the chance to do his work if only it would keep him at a distance.

Black Rafe had made no move so far to break the truce he had offered. He did not speak to Rom when they were together in the Playhouse, only looked at him with such a look of evil planning it turned Rom cold and set him shaking with dread of the time Rafe would decide to take revenge for laughter. But Rom would not tell all this to Polly and when he ordered her not to report Rafe to Old Hallam, she agreed, but she agreed reluctantly and with a long, questioning look at him.

On a Saturday in October, a day when there was no play, Rom came in sight of the Playhouse to see the whole Company assembled in their finest clothes, waiting outside the door. They were a gay sight. The women's full, light-flowered skirts swung gracefully as they moved and the men looked very grand in their dark, full-skirted coats, light-colored breeches, and three-cornered hats. Mr. Rigby even had a black cane with a silver head. Rom wondered where they were bound in their finery.

He stopped and stood where he was for a moment, admiring them, proud to be a small part of such a fine Company, heart full with a sense of belonging to them. He saw Adam leave the crowd and come running to meet him. Adam had, since the gift of sweets, attached himself to Rom and tagged after him whenever it was possible. He was, at times, a sore trouble, but Rom had not the heart to send the unhappy child away.

"Rom," Adam called as he ran, "Rom. Have you heard? There's to be a great horse race and we're invited and we're all going. Every one of us. The whole Company. You too, Rom. Hurry!"

Rom put an arm around the boy. He tried not to show his envy. A horse race! *How* he would like to see it. But he said, "Likely not me, Adam. I'm but a snuffles, you know."

Adam wriggled to free himself and stamped his foot. "No *matter*, Rom. Papa said *everybody* and you are *somebody* even if you are only a snuffles and you are too expected to go."

Rom sighed, "Come, Adam. You'll be late."

"I'll not go without you, Rom," Adam declared, tears spilling down his face.

Rom wondered what to do. Best take Adam to his father and let Old Hallam attend to this problem. He looked to find the Hallams in the group and could not see them. He took Adam's hand but Adam held back. "I won't go a step unless you promise."

"But, Adam, if I'm not invited . . ."

"You *are* invited. You are. You are. You are, I tell you. If you don't believe me, ask Jack Adcock or Pat."

"Very well. We'll do that."

Maybe if he heard Pat say no, Adam would be satisfied. Malone was standing apart from the rest and they went toward him.

"Pat," Rom began, but Adam dropped his hand and grabbed Malone about the legs and cried up to him, "Rom says he's not invited to the horse racing. But he is, Pat, isn't he? My father said everybody and Rom's somebody so he is invited. He is. He is. *You* invite him properly, Pat."

Patrick Malone gently removed the clinging arms. "For sure, he's invited, Adam. Colonel Littleton, who has long been a friend of Lewis Hallam's, Rom, sent word early this morning that his horse will run in the race today and Lewis was to bring along any who cared to come. And indeed I doubt you'd need an invitation to watch the running since it's free to all. Still, an invitation may have its own advantages. We'll see. Lewis is not free to go himself today and he has made me his deputy in this matter." He looked at Adam and made a deep bow to Rom, "I have the honor, Romulus Hormsby, to extend to you an invitation to this day's races. Will that do, Adam?"

"Will it, Rom?" Adam looked up into Rom's face as if he were asking for his life. "Will you come with us, Rom?"

"*Will* I?" Rom said, and danced a small jig before them all.

"We'd best be going then," Pat said. "Ahoy! The Company. Time!"

CHAPTER TEN

Rom thought he had never in his life known such excitement. It filled his mind and tightened all the nerves and muscles in his body and almost choked the air from his lungs. Everything was a marvel. Everything had a happy and glowing look: the sky, the sun that seemed to shine with a special golden light; the red and yellow leaves among the dark green of the pines; the cheerful people chattering together in groups or standing in twos or threes, heads together, discussing the merits of the horses and making bets on the outcome of the race.

Patrick Malone, with Adam riding high on his shoulders and Rom walking beside them, moved in and out among the groups, paying no attention to the ladies whispering, "Look! There go the Comedians!" But other bits of conversation interested Rom.

". . . a pistole on Colonel Byrd's Tryall."

". . . and I says there's none can outrun Tasker's mare even though she do be Maryland bred."

". . . ahrr, you'd never pick a Maryland beast to win over Jenny Cameron . . ."

". . . what money on Remus?"

"Remus! That newcomer! Not a ha'penny. Untried, I say, completely . . ."

Rom would have stopped and listened to more then had he not feared to lose Patrick in the crowd. Remus. A horse with such a name would hold special interest for him even if it were only good to pull a cart. Romulus and Remus. He laughed to himself. He wondered who might own Remus and wondering, put the horse out of his mind and turned back to watching the people.

He thought the whole town and half the county must be there. Artisans in their aprons or smocks; prentices, wild with the thought of a holiday; gentlemen and ladies, beautifully dressed and highly mannered; Negro serving-men and farmers and small boys, rubbed shoulders in the throng. Ahead of him, as the movements of the people opened holes in the crowd, he glimpsed now and then the heads of horses in the railed enclosure where they waited for the race to begin. By standing on his tiptoes to add another inch or two to his height he could see the circular track. Pat had told him about this track. It measured a mile and on it the racers would run three heats, each heat being four times round so that, in the end, the horses that stayed the course would have run twelve miles.

Patrick touched his shoulder and said, "Shall we go to the enclosure and look at the horses, Rom?"

"*Could* we?" Rom had not dared hope they could come so close.

"Aye. Advantage of an invitation from Colonel Little-ton, entirely." Pat looked about him for the rest of the Company and saw them scattering to talk to acquaintances among the crowd. Rom found Mrs. Adcock with

Polly in tow and knew Polly was content and forgot her. Pat turned sharply to the right and made his way toward the enclosure with Rom at his heels. When they came to the gate in the rail fence that surrounded the horses, Malone took out a single sheet of paper and showed it to the man stationed there as guard. The guard read the writing, looked carefully at the signature, and beckoned them through. "It's Enoch Brown you'll be wanting, master," he said, "there by the light bay with the white stockings and star. Colonel Littleton's man, Enoch is."

Rom followed Pat by instinct. His eyes were on the horses standing about the enclosure. He counted five; a chestnut horse, two dark bay mares and one bay horse, and the light bay with the white markings. They were all beautiful animals: long in the body, legs, and neck; full fifteen hands in height; with a look of pride and endurance. Once, in England, when he had been resting near a racing grounds, he had seen horses sired by the descendants of the great Arabian stallions, The Byerly Turk and The Darly Arabian, and he guessed that these five now before him came from the same stock which made them true thoroughbreds.

They came to the light bay and the man beside it. The man was short and compact with bow legs and skin burned until it almost matched the color of the animal beside him. His gray eyes looked worried as he closed the cover on a heavy silver watch and put it back in his pocket. Patrick told him who they were and he welcomed them in Colonel Littleton's name. "I do not know, sir, what can be keeping the Colonel. By rights he should have been here long since."

Rom had been making friends with the horse, which now put his head into Rom's shoulder and blew gently. At the sound, Enoch Brown turned from searching the road that led to the race ground. "Lord have mercy on us," he said. "What have you been doing to our Remus, lad, to charm him to you? He's not a horse to take kindly to strangers."

"Remus." Rom laughed. "Maybe he likes me because I'm Romulus."

Enoch smiled thinly at the joke. "I doubt the horse knows it. And even if he did it would take more, likely, than a name to win our Remus's affection so quickly. You've a way with horses, lad."

"I do love them," Rom said, a little embarrassed by the attention. "And indeed I've not often seen so fine a creature."

"Then you know good horseflesh, too. Remus's sire was Bulle Rocke and *his* sire was The Byerly Turk, himself. And none can say better than that. Remus is still untried on the course and the Colonel does not expect him—or for the matter of that, want him—to win this day. But some day he'll run away with any race. Do you know how to ride, Romulus?"

"I can manage," Rom said modestly, and Enock nodded. "Thought as much. You have the look of a horseman about you. Good hands. And good legs, too."

He turned from Rom and peered again at the road. A sorrel horse was coming at speed along it and the worry was again in Enoch's eyes as he shaded them against the sun. "There's trouble coming," he muttered to himself.

The rider of the sorrel jumped his horse over the fence and reined him hard and came on at a walk to Enoch.

"What is it, boy? What's amiss?" Enoch asked.

"The Colonel says," the boy began, and stopped to ease his breathing. "The Colonel says tell you Master Johnson's took bad again. He did send to the Colonel and the Colonel's gone to him. Says tell you to find a rider for Remus, for he'll sure not be here in time himself. Says Remus got to be in this race because . . ."

"I know the because," Enoch barked at him, "but where in the name of the old devil himself the Colonel expects me to find a rider and the race not a quarter hour to starting time. . . ."

He stopped in mid-sentence and looked at Rom, running his eyes once more over Rom's long legs, examining his hands, estimating his weight. Rom stood very still, guessing what was in Enoch's mind and struggling not to let his wild hope show in his eyes.

"You, Romulus," Enoch said. "Do you think you could ride Remus?"

Rom put his hand on Remus's withers and felt the light tremor as the horse responded to his touch. "Yes," Rom said, and held his breath.

Enoch gave him another long look. "We'll chance it and pray you're not overconfident."

Rom wanted to tell of some of the horses he'd ridden, but did not, fearing to sound boastful. He knew he was not overconfident. He knew Remus had accepted him, had recognized the special quality he had with animals. Remus trusted him and nothing else mattered.

"I will ride him gladly, sir," Rom said, and Enoch Brown said, "Come quickly then. My boots should fit you and I've a spare pair in the shed."

Rom wondered why Enoch did not ride himself and saw, as they moved to the shedlike structure, that the arm Enoch had, until now, held behind him, was only half an arm. No one in such a case could hope to race a young and mettlesome horse. Pity for Enoch Brown obscured, for a moment, Rom's own pleasure.

Enoch went into the shed and Rom, ready to follow, looked back once more at Remus and saw from the corner of his eye Black Rafe standing near Malone and Adam and the horse. What was Black Rafe doing here? Rom was forced to answer his own question with another. If one snuffles were included in Colonel Littleton's invitation why not the other? Rafe had as much right to be here as he had himself. He didn't like it but . . .

He heard Enoch calling and went into the shed and saw

him holding a pair of boots. While Rom was putting them on and while they were walking back to Remus, Enoch kept up a stream of instructions. It wasn't likely Remus would show signs of winning the race since he'd never been upon a real track before. Still, Rom was light in weight compared to the heavy gentlemen who would ride the other horses, and Remus was to be held back if he showed signs of taking the lead of the field. This was a schooling race for Remus, a chance to get him used to track conditions. They would take him out after the first heat. The Colonel and his friends were placing no bets today and likely nor was anyone else. Today Remus would run only for experience. Then he would be ready to make a real race at the winter fair for the purse and betting money. Rom must watch the other riders. They'd likely kick and whip him and try to unhorse him by twining their legs with his. There were no rules in these races and everyone riding wanted, above all else, to keep as many horses as possible from finishing the first heat. Rom must, on no account, let this happen to Remus.

To all of it Rom nodded. He was already sending his mind ahead to the horse and Remus seemed to know it for he lifted his head and looked toward Rom and whinnied a welcome.

Patrick Malone and Adam had gone, likely to find places near the course. There was no sign of Rafe, and Rom was relieved. He had no wish to be distracted by the sight of Rafe's leering face.

Enoch tested the reins and the saddle girth and swore when Remus, who had been standing quietly enough, suddenly kicked out viciously and snorted. "Now what in the name of the devil?" Enoch asked. Rom spoke softly into the horse's ear and rubbed his nose and Remus was, at once, quiet. The other horses were already heading toward the starting line. Enoch said, "Nervous, likely. Up you go, Romulus."

Rom tugged a little at the saddle to settle it more to his

liking before he mounted. Remus screamed and reared, shaking off Rom's hand and almost knocking him over. The next moment the horse was quiet again, standing still and nuzzling Rom's shoulder as if asking his pardon for such rude behavior. Enoch Brown was speaking angrily, but Rom did not hear the words.

He was thinking of Rafe, guessing Rafe had been up to some mischief with the horse. "Stand to his head, Mr. Brown," Rom said, and loosened the girth and probed gently beneath the saddle until he found what he had suspected. He brought out his hand and showed Enoch Brown a chestnut still in its prickly green burr.

"Now, how in tarnation," Enoch began, but Rom said, "No time now. Help me with the girth," and put the burr in his pocket while Enoch rammed his head into Remus's side and tightened the girth again.

A sounding trumpet floated clearly above the crowd noises and Enoch held the stirrup for Rom. He swung himself into the saddle and Remus turned his head and whin-

nied softly and Rom spoke sweetly in his ear and patted
his neck.

"Good luck, Romulus, and remember what I've told
you." Enoch Brown's face was angry as Rom headed
Remus toward the start of the course. He had just time
to take his place before the final trumpet sounded and five
horses began the first heat of the long race.

Rom never afterward forgot that day. It remained clear
in his mind when many more important things had been
long forgotten. Remus was one with the wind, running as
if he would prove with willing speed that his ill behavior
had been caused only by pain. Rom had all he could do to
hold the horse from taking the lead and keeping it. He
had only a sense of the crowd, a sense of color and shouts
and excitement. He saw a whip aimed at his shoulder and
swerved to avoid it. Another rider began to crowd him,
trying to force Remus off the track. Remus snorted and
started to run out and Rom tightened the rein to steady
him and kicked the other rider in the leg so that he gave

over crowding. Remus steadied and kept on running. They came around the starting line for the last lap of the heat and Rom caught a single glimpse of Enoch Brown and beside him Patrick still holding Adam on his shoulders and all of them with their mouths open, shouting. One of the horses had dropped far behind and was ridden off the course and out of the race, but the others were still running.

Rom thought he would have given all he had to ride Remus all the way to win, but he remembered his instructions and, when they neared the starting line for the fourth time, he began to pull at the reins and dropped behind the three leaders and turned Remus toward the enclosure. Enoch was there before him, his face split in a wide grin. He called for a stableboy to walk Remus home to his own stall and pounded Rom on the back saying over and over, "Good boy! Good boy! Good boy! What a horse! What a horse!" until he had no breath left.

They went, then, to the shed so Rom could change back into his own shoes. "Now, Romulus," Enoch said, "you'll come straightaway to Colonel Littleton himself and have his own thanks for your courtesy and good riding."

Rom shook his head. "I doubt it's a time to be bothering your Colonel Littleton. It's I should be doing the thanking for the pleasure I've had in riding such a horse as Remus. You'll oblige me if you'll not mention me at all to your Colonel."

"Now as to that," Enoch Brown said, "you know I must say something. The Colonel will be asking me first thing who rode our Remus."

"Then I do beg you, tell him only that you found a person who could ride, and did, and that is all you know. Anyway it will be the horse he's interested in, not me."

He hated to be thanked. Standing about while someone told his gratitude made him shy and awkward. He wanted none of it. Enoch Brown said, reluctantly, "Very well,

Romulus. If you want it so. Had it not been for you we'd have had no chance to see our Remus run. Still . . ."

"Thank you, Mr. Brown," Rom said before Enoch could change his mind. "Now I must be off to my friends. Maybe you'll let me come to see Remus now and again."

"Whenever you will and as often as you will. Anybody in Williamsburg can tell you where to find Colonel Little-ton's stables. We'll be at the town house now till after Twelfth-night. You're sure you won't . . ."

But Rom was already moving away from him. He turned at the door to wave good-by and put his hand in his pocket and felt the chestnut burr. The running of the race had put it right out of his mind. As he went to find Patrick Malone he closed his fingers gently over it and felt the sting of the spines and knew what pain Remus must have felt from the much harder pressure of the saddle.

Black Rafe had done this cruel thing. Rom knew it as if he had himself seen the chestnut slipped cunningly under the saddle where it would hurt only when pressed upon. Rafe must have overheard Enoch's plans for Rom to ride and hoped to do him serious hurt. He vowed that, some-how, some time, he would make Rafe Bascomb pay for his cruelties.

CHAPTER ELEVEN

October stretched into November and Rom did nothing to punish Rafe and hated himself that he did not. Each Monday and Wednesday and Friday he watched Rafe across the Theater and promised himself that this night he would surely do what he knew he should do, and each time the curtain descended to mark the end of the play he left the Playhouse quickly and went, almost furtively, back to the caravan. He could not even take pleasure in the stories that came to life upon the stage. He heard the laughter of the audience when the evening's performance was a comedy by Mr. Farquhar and felt their rapt attention when Mrs. Hallam acted the part of one of Shakespeare's tragic heroines. But his own mind was busy with shame and he gave little heed to the stage.

And he had lost again the small warm feeling of belonging that had begun to grow in the loneliness of his
mind.

On the afternoon of the tenth of November he came to
the Playhouse feeling even more disgusted with himself
than usual. Adam met him at the door and Rom made an
effort to throw away his gloom, for he had become fond of
the child and liked to do whatever he could to bring some
pleasure into his life, so often made miserable by his older
brother.

Adam began at once to talk at top speed. He spoke so
rapidly his words ran together and Rom could make nothing of them. "Do you slow down a mite, Adam," he said,
smiling down at the small boy. "I can scarce tell one
word from the next. Now do you begin again and speak
it slowly and plain."

Adam gulped and began again. "It's the Indians, Rom.
Have you not heard? The King and Queen of the Cherokee Nation are come with a whole company of redskinned
men to speak with the Governor. They are dressed in
strange clothes and they do be coming to the play tonight
and my father is running about and about and pulling at
his hair—he does look funny, Rom, when he does so—and
moaning and groaning . . ."

He'd been speaking faster and faster as he went along,
and Rom put a hand on his shoulder and pressed it hard.
"Adam, Adam," he said—very slowly, to calm the young-
ster with his own calm—"you're fair galloping again. Hold
up a minute and let me get this straightened out. These
Cherokees are coming to see us do *Othello* tonight. And
your father is running about and moaning. Why, young
Adam? Does your father not want us to play for the Indian visitors?"

"No, goose," Adam said. "My father is upset because
Mr. Rigby was supposed to speak the prologue and he's
gone and caught a quinsy and when he says something it
comes out all croaking and my father says there do be

no time for another to learn the prologue lines that are all written specially for this night and he'll not have them read from a paper not with that redskin King and Queen listening and my father does not know *what* he'll do so as not to be disgraced and . . ."

He stopped to draw a breath and Rom said, quickly, "Well, and why not just have the show without a prologue?"

Adam looked at him scornfully. "Who ever heard of such a thing, Rom? There always *has* to be a prologue. There just naturally always *is*. Nobody ever heard of beginning a play without a *prologue*."

"Oh." Rom felt a little foolish seeing Adam's obvious disbelief that he could have made such a suggestion. "Well come along with me now. May be something's already been thought of and your father will be calm again."

But when they made their way below stage they found only turmoil. Nobody had thought of a solution. Old Hallam was indeed tearing his hair out in handfuls and rushing about and talking to himself. They would have to open without a prologue and who ever heard of such a thing. No play had opened on the first line of the script in his memory. There was *always* a prologue, written for the occasion, and here they were with royalty—albeit only Indian royalty—and not even an old one that could be dressed up and made to do, for without Rigby there was no one who could get up even those few lines in the time left. What would the good people of Williamsburg think, let alone this King and Queen of the Cherokee Nation? How could he face his friends again after such discourtesy to the audience? Oh woe! Oh woe! Oh woe!

"What *is* going on, Rom?"

Polly had come unprepared upon the scene. She was holding Desdemona's costume and she stood beside Rom with a comical look of bewilderment upon her face. Rom explained and saw her eyes begin to sparkle and thought she was up to some mischief.

"Oh that!" she said. "That's easily mended. Here hold this."

She pushed the costume into Rom's hands and went across the greenroom to Old Hallam and took his sleeve. He did not stop his pacing and broke off moaning only long enough to say, "Be off with you, girl. No time for costumes now. No time."

Polly hung on. "Will you but listen a moment, sir? About the prologue. I've a plan."

"Plan! Plan! What plan, girl? Speak up. Speak up."

She bent close to him and whispered in his ear. The harassed look left his face and a small smile began to grow where it had been. He looked at Rom and back at Polly and said aloud, "He does, does he? Who would have guessed it?" and looked again toward Rom. "That might do it. Yes. It just might. Snuffles! Come here at once."

Rom started forward and found his legs tangled in the folds of Desdemona's gown still dangling from his arms and almost fell upon his face and caught himself just in time. He looked around wildly for someone to hand the dress to and ended by winding it about his own neck as he went across the room to Old Hallam. Adam tagged along behind, holding up the hem of the dress.

"Do you know all William Shakespeare's prologues, Snuffles? Word perfect?" Old Hallam asked.

"Well—yes, sir. That I do. But *Othello*, sir? There's no prologue to *Othello*."

"Think I don't know that? Teach an old dog his tricks, would you?" Old Hallam's voice was testy, but his eyes were smiling. "What about *King Henry V*? What about that, eh? Wouldn't it do, now? Wouldn't it? With a little cutting? It'll be the very thing, eh?"

Rom nodded.

"Then, Rom Hormsby, do you go and cut it and quickly, too." Old Hallam cocked his head on one side, listening. "No time to be lost. No time at all. Gallery seats already filling up."

"Me, sir?" Rom asked. "I—I don't think I understand you, sir."

"What ails you then, Snuffles? Do I not speak plain enough? You are to go quickly and think on the Prologue to *King Henry V* by Master William Shakespeare and cut out all that refers to that play alone and don suitable clothes—someone will lend you a proper costume—and go out before the curtain and speak the prologue."

Rom felt dizzy. He wondered if he could just remember the words. Suppose he forgot in the middle! Suppose he did not cut the lines properly. There wasn't enough time. He couldn't do it. He knew he couldn't. "But, sir, the candles . . ." he began, but Old Hallam cut him short. "My problem. Other Snuffles attend to all. He's strong enough, forsooth. Now do you stop wasting time. And do you, Adam, get up the stairs and ask Mr. Pelham if he will kindly entertain our guests with music on the harpsichord until I give the word to stop. And send the other Snuffles to me, Adam. Get along now, fast, young sprout, and do you, Rom Hormsby, hurry with your cutting and your dressing and stop standing as if you've taken a fit. Mr. Pelham cannot hold this crowd forever. And give that costume to your sister before it strangles you."

Rom heard the voice but not the words. His mind was already busy with the lines of the prologue. He hardly knew when Polly unwound Desdemona's gown from his neck and Patrick Malone took him in charge and changed his claret-colored duffel clothes for white satin breeches and scarlet waistcoat and a white coat sprigged all over with green. Patrick stripped off brown thread stockings and plain brown shoes and replaced them with white silk and handsome black leather with pinchbeck buckles. He handed Rom a three-cornered hat and said, "Do you turn about and about, Rom, so I may see if you'll do."

Rom did as he was told, as if he were sleep-walking. His lips moved, repeating the prologue. Patrick adjusted the fine lawn ruffles at his wrists and removed a speck of lint from the coat.

"Get along now, lad, and don't forget to speak out loud and clear. And luck go with you, Romulus Hormsby. You do be a very proper figure of a man."

Rom was shaking so hard he could scarcely hold the hat. "I can't, Patrick," he said, and heard his voice creak in his throat. "I can't. I'll forget the words. All those *faces*, Pat! I'll misspeak myself and disgrace us all."

Patrick grinned at him. "That you'll not, Rom. You've a bit of the stage fright on you now and that's all to the good entirely. It will pass. It will pass. You'll see. Do you trust Patrick."

He led the shaking Rom up the steps to the stage and nodded to Old Hallam waiting in the wings. Hallam whispered to Adam beside him and Adam disappeared. A few minutes later the music ceased and Patrick said, "On you go, Rom," and started him toward the stage.

Rom thought he must turn and run. He could not go out on that empty stage and face all those people and speak Old Will Shakespeare's lines. He stood entirely still, his mind empty of the well-known words, his legs refusing to carry him forward, and in the seconds that this was so he heard Polly's voice behind him. "It's no worse than the Little People, Rom. Besides Papa's out front. I sent a messenger for him. Don't you dare keep him waiting after I've gone to all the trouble of getting him here."

Rom pushed back his shoulders and stepped out before the curtain.

The audience applauded politely, and he looked out at row upon row of white faces staring at him and he could not make a sound. Then Papa's face came clear among the others. Papa was looking straight into his eyes and smiling and making with his right hand their private sign of encouragement. Rom forgot to be afraid and when the applause lessened he made a deep and graceful bow, sud-

denly conscious of how fine he must look in his splendid
borrowed clothes, and began to speak the words:

"O for a Muse of fire, that would ascend
The brightest heaven of invention . . ."

His voice, a little husky at first, grew clear and strong
as he got the first two lines behind him. He found himself

moving easily about the stage and gesturing easily as he spoke. He felt outside himself, as if he were one of the Little People and someone else were pulling the strings. Why, there's nothing to it, he thought.

> "A kingdom for a stage, princes to act
> And monarchs to behold the swelling scene!
> O, pardon! since a crooked figure may
> Attest in little place a million;
> And let us, ciphers to this great accompt,
> On your imaginary forces work."

He moved downstage and heard a hissing and saw Rafe making hideous, threatening faces at him and stumbled in the speech. He had a sense that everyone in the house, everyone except Rafe, was leaning toward him, straining to help him as if each were his particular friend and he loved each of them in that instant for their good will. He took a deep breath, fighting swift panic. He forced himself to look away from Rafe and found Papa's face again and caught up the next words boldly and triumphantly and went on to the end without a blunder.

> "Piece out our imperfections with your thoughts;
> Into a thousand parts divide one man,
> And make imaginary puissance;
> Think, when we talk of horses, that you see them
> Printing their proud hoofs i' the receiving earth;
> For 'tis your thoughts that now must deck our kings,
> Carry them here and there; jumping o'er times,
> Turning the accomplishment of many years
> Into an hour-glass: for the which supply,
> Admit me Chorus to this history;
> Who prologue-like your humble patience pray,
> Gently to hear, kindly to judge, our play."

When he had done and was again hidden behind the protecting wings of the stage the noise of clapping hands followed him in a wave of approval. He heard the curtain going up and the whispers of congratulation from the members of the Company as if they came from a great distance, for his mind was still filled with the sounding beauty of the poetry.

Old Hallam caught his arm and steered him toward the stairs. When they were again below the stage Hallam said, "Well done, Rom. It's clear you've the heart of an actor. It may be we can do something about teaching you the craft before our season is closed here."

Rom wondered if he had heard properly. Had Hallam promised to try to teach him to be an actor? He knew suddenly that this would answer the loneliness in his heart, that the theater would be for him a fitting habitation and a home, but he could not think more about it now for Old Hallam had asked him a question.

"Sir?"

"I asked what caused that stumble in the middle of the speech, Rom."

Rom hesitated, trying to decide quickly whether or not to tell Old Hallam about Rafe. It did not take him long to make up his mind. If Rom Hormsby could not fight his own battles, he'd not go squealing like a pig to another. "It—it was just that the words—those I'd cut out, sir—wanted to push in again. I—I am sorry. I hope it—it did no harm."

"No harm at all, Rom," Old Hallam reassured him. "I did but wonder why you stumbled. And, indeed, you've made all clear. You'd best get into your own clothes and go back to your candles now. We'll talk about your future later, but you may be sure we'll find a way. You're too good a natural actor to waste."

The play was moving smoothly when Rom took up his station as snuffles. He had learned to keep an ear cocked for his calls and at the same time give his attention to the play, but tonight he took some time to examine the Cherokees in the Governor's box. The King and Queen and their young son sat in unmoving dignity. A number of men and women of their nation stood behind them, not shifting so much as a foot, not taking their eyes from the stage. Rom could not see them clearly for the shadows in the boxes, but he had an impression of a circlet of shells and scarlet fringe. As he watched, the Queen suddenly sat forward, tensely, her eyes on the stage, her mouth opened. Rom turned to look where she looked and saw that two of the actors were playing at fighting a duel and looked back again at the Cherokee Queen wondering what had caught her attention. She was turning now to speak to the warriors behind her and he moved, curious, until he was under the box and could hear what she said. She was commanding her braves to stop the fight in order to prevent the actors from killing one another!

Rom felt laughter rising in him, but at the same time, he realized that if the warriors did as she bade them it would ruin the play and he wondered what he should do. Then he saw that Old Hallam, waiting in the wings close under the box, had also heard the Queen and was already going to explain. Rom turned back to the stage.

When the play and the Harlequin pantomime which followed it were over the whole audience followed the Cherokee embassy out into Palace Street where Mr. Hallam had promised a show of fireworks. Rom, watching with Papa and Polly, from the outskirts of the crowd, caught his breath at the brilliance of the scene. The whole town was illuminated as if for the King's Birthday with candles in all the windows and the great lanthorn atop the Governor's Palace blazing with light. Many ladies and gentlemen waited in the frosty air, splendid in furs and silks and satins that sparkled with all the colors he had ever imagined. The Governor and his Indian guests stood upon the steps of the Palace and everybody's eyes were turned toward them until the first of the fireworks shot, hissing, into the sky over the Market Square and blossomed out into the picture of a galleon in full sail, which hung a moment against the black sky before its colors faded and its outlines dimmed into darkness. When the display was over, elegant ladies and their gentlemen went to the Governor's Palace to attend a ball, and Rom and Polly, with Papa, his limp more marked than usual because the night air was damp and he was tired, went quietly back to the caravan.

The next day was a holiday for the Hallam Company and, when breakfast was over and Papa had gone off happily to the printing office, Rom said, "Polly do you come with me for I've a secret thing to show you."

"What, Rom? What kind of thing?"

"Do you come along and ask no questions."

He grinned at her, thinking of her delight when he showed her the hut he'd found hidden in the forest and made useful again in secret during his spare hours. He had decided last night he wanted to share it with her, and he had been hardly able to wait for the morning.

He had repaired the door of the hut with a pair of bent, discarded hinges he'd begged from the blacksmith and hammered back into shape. Now the hut was tight and sound, the door locked and the key in his pocket, and he was in a swivet to show it to her.

"Where are we going then, Rom?" she asked.

"You'll see, my lass, you'll see," he answered, enjoying teasing her.

She stamped her foot. "I'll not go a step until you tell me. Besides," she added, not really wanting to spoil his surprise whatever it was, "I only want to know if we will pass the Playhouse. I left my thimble there last night and I'll need it before the day is out."

"Yes," Rom said, "we will go the long way round and stop for your thimble and come home by the short path. Do come along now."

The day was fair and warm though it was November, and the air was sweet. Rom said he'd wait outside while she fetched the thimble. He had hardly settled himself to watch a pair of squirrels at play on the edge of the forest

128

when he heard her calling and saw her running toward him. Her face was red as a turkey's wattles and her voice was shrill.

"Come! Come quickly, Rom."

"What is it, Polly?" His spine was prickling with a fear he could not put a name to. It was not like Polly to be easily upset and now her face was white and she was breathing as if she had run many miles.

She caught his hand and dragged him after her. "It's Adam," she said.

"What about Adam?"

"Don't *talk*, Rom. Save your breath and hurry. You'll see."

Rom thought there was little use in speaking further. She'd have her way whatever it was, but he wondered why she would not tell him what was amiss.

She dropped his hand and ran before him down the steps that led beneath the stage. Rom came after her, hard put to it to match her speed, and almost collided with her when she pulled up short at the door of the greenroom. The room was shadowy and at first Rom could not see what it was Polly pointed toward. But he could hear. He could hear Adam whimpering in pain or fear and even as his eyes began to adjust to the semi-dark he went toward the sound, calling out, "It's Rom, Adam. I'm coming. Don't be afraid."

"So, you're coming, coward," Rafe Bascomb said, and sounded amused. "And what, think you, will come of that? 'Don't be afraid.'" He mimicked Rom's voice and twisted Adam's arm again and Adam cried out and Rom felt wrath such as he'd never known before. He was so angry he had no room for thought or for fear. The two figures before him swam in a fine red mist and he charged forward and swung his doubled fist at Rafe.

The blow was not well aimed and it just grazed Rafe's forehead, bringing no pain, but Rafe dropped Adam's arm and the boy ran to Polly, still whimpering. At another time

Rom would have laughed at the look of unbelieving surprise upon Rafe's face, but now there was no space in him for laughter and no time.

Rafe roared and swung at him and missed, and Rom hit back. Again and again they sought to land their separate blows. Neither of them knew anything of the science of fighting, but Rafe's greater size and strength were telling against Rom. Rom heard Adam and Polly calling encouragement and felt the pain from Rafe's fists on his face and body and did not care. His only care, indeed, was to keep on fighting, to keep from tiring until, somehow, he could teach Black Rafe Bascomb a lesson, could repay him for the hours of terror and shame, for the burr under Remus's saddle, and for Adam's twisted arm.

He saw Rafe's foot raised to kick him and twisted aside, aiming another blow in Rafe's general direction. By luck it cracked against Rafe's nose and started a stream of blood from it. Rafe's kick, going wide of its mark, had thrown him off balance and he fell upon his back with a thump. Rom, winded and desperately tired, stepped aside, taking great breaths into his lungs, wondering whether he would be able to lift his hands when Rafe got up and came at him again. Waiting, he had a moment to think that no matter what the outcome of the fight he'd never again know the kind of fear he'd lived with so long and he wondered why he had ever been afraid.

Rafe did not get up.

He lay on his back, looking at his own hands, covered with the blood he'd started to wipe away from his nose. And he blubbered. He blubbered as if he had been younger and more timorous than Adam.

For a space of sixty heartbeats Rom looked at him, waiting still, not believing what his eyes saw. Rafe Bascomb, shivering and weeping because of a bloody nose! It just couldn't possibly be true. For all Rom's efforts, there was no other mark upon him. Surely, Rom thought, conscious of half a hundred aching spots on his own body, surely big, strong, blustering Rafe was not defeated by a bloody nose!

Rom moved at last—slowly for he was bone-tired, but gladly in his new-found confidence in himself. He stood above Rafe and poked at him with the toe of his shoe. "Get up, Black Rafe Bascomb," he said, "get up and let us finish this fight between us. I've yet to repay you for the trick you put upon Remus or, enough, for tormenting young Adam."

Rafe did not, for a moment, move at all. He lay upon the floor and looked first at Rom and then at his blood-covered hands, and there was fear in his look. Rom nudged him again with his foot and Rafe cried out and rolled away and got to his knees. "Let me alone," he whined. "Let me alone you—you coward."

Rom laughed.

"You—you made my nose bleed. You—you—leave me be, I say. Or—or I'll—I'll tell Mr. Hallam."

Rom laughed again. "I'll not keep you, Rafe Bascomb. I've no wish to be looking longer at your ugly face. And it's plain you'll not fight again this day. But"—his voice hardened and rose in a kind of joy at his own deliverance from himself—"if I ever again so much as hear a whisper that you've bothered young Adam—or yet any horse in this town—I'll bloody more than your nose. Now *get!*"

CHAPTER TWELVE

Rom hurried toward the town. It was very late. He shivered and blamed himself that he had waited so long to leave the Struthers's farm where he had gone partly for a visit, partly to make arrangements for a stable for Betsy and a shed for the caravan during the winter.

All through November the fine weather had held, but this first week of December had turned cold and it had become clear to them all that they could not stay much longer, in comfort, in the caravan. Tomorrow they would take up lodgings in the town, lodgings which Dr. Hay had found for them in the house of the Widow Dawson.

So, after supper, Rom had gone to the Struthers's, and Mrs. Struthers had bade him stay and he had lingered overlong, helping her boil myrtleberry leaves for wax she would shape into sweet-smelling candles. When he had finally left, his mind had been taken up with Polly's craft in freeing him from his fear of Black Rafe. He had been thinking again, as he often had during the weeks just past, of what she had told him as she washed and bandaged the cuts and bruises he'd brought home to the caravan from his fight, while Adam, his misery forgotten, played with an old, small cat puppet of Rom's making.

"Why did you not tell me at once that Rafe was tormenting Adam?" Rom had asked, and Polly had looked at him and said nothing until he had repeated the question and added, "I should then have been the better prepared to fight Rafe."

"Would you so, Rom?" she had asked slowly, and he had felt the blood come into his face and turned his head away from her quickly.

"Hold still, Rom," she had ordered him. "How can I mend your hurts if you twist about and about? You've no cause to blush like a love-sick girl. Anybody will, of right, be afraid if they've time to think on it. I well knew you would be a very catamountain for bravery in Adam's defense. If you had no time to think."

"B-b-but," he had stammered, and swallowed and started again. "But, Polly, how could you know about—about my fears?"

"How could I not, Rom, being your twin and in the strange ways of twins, knowing your heart as you know mine. I've always known of your fears and found no time till now to prove them false to you. Known as I know now you are still shamed by the past though you've no cause to be. Why *must* men creatures be ever blaming themselves if they do not revel in quarreling? You do but want to live peaceably, Rom, and avoid useless blows. What do you see shameful in that?"

He shook his head, wondering. In truth, as she said it, there was nothing shameful. And yet he had felt shamed. "I—," he began, and shook his head again and said, "Nothing shameful, I reckon, Polly. At least not now. Not so long as I know I'll not run from a fight if there is good and true cause for it."

"Yes," she said, "so I knew. And was glad for a chance

133

to prove you to yourself, though I'd not have chosen young Adam as cause for the proving."

Tonight—thinking of her wisdom and thanking her in his heart for the thousandth time; thinking, too, of his own new-found freedom from shame and fear—he had missed the turning into the wood path and wasted time in retracing his way for upwards of two miles. And now he guessed it was after eleven of the clock and he was cold and Papa and Polly would likely be fretting and he could cheerfully have kicked himself.

He came abreast of the Playhouse almost running and had all but gone by it when his eyes registered the fact of a light inside. Some careless fool, probably Rafe, had left a candle burning. A lighted candle was dangerous in the frame building. It could fire the whole place if it happened to be in the right spot to catch the painted scenery or the curtain. He'd best go put it out. He hoped the door would not be locked for he had no key, and hoping, came to it and saw it swinging wide and heard a low moaning sound as if someone were in pain, and hurried across the anteroom and into the pit.

A single candle was burning in one of the hanging circles and by its light he could just make out some kind of dark mass on the spikes that shielded the stage. The moans had stopped and the Theater was deathstill as he stood for a space, not breathing, fearing to know more. When he shook himself free of the strange dread and ran toward the stage, he saw that the huddled, dark thing was a man.

He snatched a candle from his store of replacements and fumbled in his pocket for his tinderbox. It took his shaking fingers a full minute to make a light and when he had the candle held high above the injured man he almost dropped it, for the man was Patrick Malone, beaten and cast upon the iron guard so that one of the spikes had pierced the calf of his leg.

He had, Rom saw and was glad, fainted, and was, for the moment, not conscious of his own suffering. Rom knew

134

help was needed, yet he could not rouse his mind to seek it until he heard a thread of song through the open doors. He ran then and saw in the faint starlight two men passing the Playhouse, singing softly together

> "I'm a-rolling, I'm a-rolling,
> I'm a-rolling along in an unfriendly world
> I'm a-rolling . . ."

"Help!" Rom shouted at the top of his voice. "Come and help me!"

The singing stopped in the middle of a word, and one of the men turned and saw Rom, the candle still in his hand, and said something to his companion.

"Hurry!" Rom called, and the two men moved toward him quickly and he saw that one of them was little older than he.

"What's amiss, young master?" the older of the two asked.

"A man's been hurt. Inside. Come," Rom answered, already leading the way inside.

"God Almighty!" the two men said in unison when they saw Pat.

"Help me!" Rom was almost sobbing. "Help me get him off those spikes."

"Easy now," the older man said. "Maybe we'd best send for doctor afore we move him. Do you, Ben, fetch Dr. Hay. He do be closest. And be quick about it."

Ben nodded, and left, and Rom stood shivering. The man put his hand on Rom's arm and spoke to him gently, "How'd it happen, young master?"

"I—I don't know," Rom said and told, as well as he could for the chattering of his teeth, how he had come to find Pat.

"Do you not worry more, young master. Ben's a good boy. He'll fetch the doctor quick-like."

Even as he spoke they heard running feet and Dr. Hay,

with Ben at his heels, came into the Theater. The doctor glanced at Rom and said, "Rom! What do you here?" and did not wait for an answer but bent over Patrick and examined him as best he could.

"Is he—is he dead?" Rom asked.

"No. Battered and hurt, but not dead." Dr. Hay straightened and really looked at Rom and saw his face white and his body shaking and said sharply, "Get you home, Rom. Ben, here, and Jake will help me with Malone. There's nothing you can do."

"But," Rom started to argue.

"Do as I say, Rom. You'll only be in the way. Malone will mend, though he may take a time in doing it. Go now. Tell Mistress Polly to give you a cup of sweet, strong tea with a noggin of rum if she has it and do you then go straight to bed."

Rom was wakened next morning by Adam's shrill voice outside the caravan. He lay for a moment with his eyes still closed, feeling oppression heavy in his mind and unable, at first, to say why. Then he heard Polly asking after Patrick Malone and remembered and got quickly out of the bed and into his clothes.

Polly gave him the news of Pat with breakfast. He was weak and exhausted and would need a good long time of rest while his bruises mended and the wound in his leg healed. Dr. Hay had said it was the Lord's own blessing that the spike had not broken a bone or pierced an artery. Pat was uncomfortable, to be sure, but he was not dangerously damaged. He could tell them nothing of what had happened except that he had gone to the Playhouse after supper to refresh his memory of the part of a gravedigger in *Hamlet*, because the tenement was bedlam in the evening. He had been on the stage going through his part when three men had burst in on him and, before he could so much as get a look at their faces, had set upon him and beaten him and thrown him on the spikes and fled. He had no notion who they were or why they had attacked him.

Half a hundred questions swarmed in Rom's mind but he did not ask them for Polly insisted he eat his breakfast and Adam was plainly bursting to talk. Rom sat on his bunk and ate the corn pone and drank the milk Polly gave him and listened to Adam.

"My father says you're to come at once, Rom. He says it never rains but it pours and not only is Pat sick abed but Mr. Wynell and Mr. Herbert have disappeared and can't be found in the town and bad luck to them. My father says they are good riddance altogether, or would be if they'd not left him shorthanded, for they've done nothing but make trouble since we left England and why he ever took them into the company he can't say. So—anyway—" he paused to take a breath and Rom waited—"anyway my father says he'll have to change the play for tonight to *The Beaux' Stratagem* and you're to play the part in it usually done by Mr. Herbert."

"Me?" Rom asked. "But I can't, Adam. I don't know that play and I could never learn any part before tonight."

Adam giggled. "Yes you can, Rom. It's just a little bitty part. All you do is come on the stage and say"—he rattled off the line in one breath, without space between the words—"'Madam, my lady ordered me to tell you that your brother is below at the gate.' But my father says you're to hurry, Rom, for the whole Company must spend the best part of the day preparing."

Rom's mind was whirling. Here was a chance he'd never hoped for. He must hurry to the Playhouse. He started for his coat and stopped midway to it. But this was the day when they must move to the new lodgings. There was Betsy to see to and the caravan and . . .

"Do stop fretting, Rom," Polly said quietly. "It will not harm Betsy and the caravan to stay one night more in the field. You can take them to Struthers's on the morrow. I'll find a carter and move the Little People and our clothes

137

and things to the Widow Dawson's. Get along and leave all else to me and Papa."

"Hurry, Rom. Hurry! Hurry!" Adam chanted, jumping up and down in excitement, and Rom grabbed his coat from its peg and hugged Polly for thanks and hurried.

The Playhouse was in an uproar. Old Hallam roamed the house, cracking his knuckles and talking to himself. Men and women stood about the stage wondering excitedly who had set upon Patrick Malone and where Wynell and Herbert had gone and why. Young Lewis, keeping himself apart, had a look upon his face that seemed to say he could tell a tale about the disappearance if he had a mind to. Rom stopped in the doorway to get back the breath he had lost in running.

Wynell and Herbert, he thought. They had been quarrelsome men, with an exaggerated notion of their own talents and a searing envy of the principal players, especially Pat. Could it have been those two and some unknown third who had so cruelly mistreated Malone and then run away? Likely no one would ever know and besides there was no time to think about it now. But if he ever caught sight of them . . .

Old Hallam turned in his pacing and saw Rom and called out, "Well, Romulus, has Adam told you why I sent for you in such haste?"

"Yes, sir."

"And will you play the part for me?"

"Indeed, sir, I'll gladly try. Adam says there's but one line and I doubt I'll have trouble with that."

"Good then. In a moment we'll run through the scene and I'll show you what you are to do."

Rom turned toward the stage, and Old Hallam put out a hand and stopped him. "There'll be other times, Rom, when it's likely we'll be needing you. Wynell and Herbert, as you know, covered many small parts between them. With a bit of teaching from—well, from Pat while he's mending—you could learn those tricks of the stage you'll need for the present. So, if you're willing, we'll make you a regular member of the Company with a regular share in the profits."

"Willing, sir!" Rom's eyes shone with pleasure. "Willing? Of course I'm willing, sir. And thank you, Mr. Hallam. But—but what of the candles, sir? You'll need another snuffles."

"We'll think of that later, Rom. We'll find someone. To work now. We've little enough time to do what must be done before tonight."

Everyone worked valiantly all morning and by three o'clock Old Hallam declared himself satisfied and sent them to their dinners. Rom started for the caravan, taking the short cut through the woods in order the more quickly to tell Polly the news. He could not believe in his own good fortune, and he was pinching his arm to prove himself awake when he felt a heavy hand grasp his shoulder and spin him around to face Black Rafe. For just one breath he felt the old, familiar beginnings of fear tighten his stomach and thought he'd rejoiced too soon that Polly had set him free; had believed too easily that his physical fear could be driven away by one lucky blow in a wild fight. He looked at Rafe and saw his hands tightening and knew what was coming and wondered why he himself was not already running. Then he felt a surging triumph and knew he was not running because he was, in truth, no longer afraid.

He spread his feet a little for a firmer base and doubled his own fists in readiness. This time, he promised himself, he would give Master Rafe Bascomb more than a bloody nose. He waited, looking at his opponent with distaste, having, even now, no real stomach for this way of settling differences whatever they might be. He would not, at least, offer the first blow.

Rafe stood his ground briefly. Then he uncurled his hands and dropped his arms. Rom held his own position, thinking this could be a trick. Rafe snarled at him, teeth bared like an angry dog. "Be you not afeared, little man, Rafe'll not hurt you."

"I'm not afraid, Rafe Bascomb," Rom said quietly. "Whatever's wrong with you that you do be forever seeking me out to quarrel with me?"

Rafe's face was red with anger, but he made no more effort to fight and Rom, realizing suddenly that Rafe was, himself, a coward—and a bully—dropped his own arms and said, again, "What *is* the matter with you?"

"Matter?" Rafe said. "I'll tell you the matter, you sneaking, sniveling snuffles. Is it not enough that you laugh at my puppets and spoil my sport with young Adam? I'd never have harmed the silly little boy, only I thought to tease him a bit."

"It's not my notion of teasing," Rom said hotly, "when you . . ."

Rafe cut him off. "And now. *Now* you go sneaking like the weasel you be and making up to Old Hallam and stealing a place in the Company that should of rights be mine. Just because you've wasted your time alearning of fine speeches from plays is no reason you should be given old Wynell's parts. Arrh, yes. I was there. I heard Old Hallam. And it's not fair, it's not. *I've* been snuffles longer nor you. *I* could walk out and speak a line good as you. Likely better. But you, you sneaking, skulking, sniveling . . ."

"That's *enough*, Rafe Bascomb!" Rom's voice was loud in the still day. He took two steps toward Rafe and Rafe backed away. "I'll listen to no more of your abuse. Do you say a single word more and I'll give you what you'll not soon forget."

He turned and walked away and did not see Rafe's hating face and shaking fist. Nor did he hear the threatening words Rafe sent after him for he whispered them softly.

CHAPTER THIRTEEN

On the third day after his beating, Patrick Malone sent to ask Rom to come to the tenement. Rom went gladly, taking with him a leather purse of coins the members of the Company had contributed to help pay Dr. Hay's fee.

Pat was propped up against pillows. Where his skin showed between swathings of linen bandages, it had a greenish-pale look and his eyes still held the memory of of pain, but he was cheerful enough and he hurried to make light of Rom's troubled concern. "Don't you go fretting, Rom. Another week and I'll be well entirely. Sit down, my lad, sit down. Bring yon chair closer. I've a thing to tell you I hope will please you."

Rom brought the chair close and sat beside the bed. "Can't it wait, Pat?" he asked, thinking Malone was scarcely strong enough to talk much.

"Likely," Pat said, "but I can't. The beating had one good effect, Rom. It untied a kink in my memory."

Rom sat very still. He guessed what was coming and

wanted none of it. He realized he had not, for weeks, given thought to his real father, and now the very mention of Pat's returning memory was enough to bedevil him again. He'd much rather not listen but you couldn't argue with a man who looked so ill and tired. He tried to prepare himself for what might be coming and hoped his feelings did not show in his face and said, "Did it now, Pat?"

"That it did. The very next morning when I came to myself in my own bed, looking, I've no doubt, like one of those Egyptian mummies I've heard of, the first thing popped into my mind was that benefit ticket of yours and at once I remembered all about it. You mind I told you that benefit was held in the town of Bath, and a fine old place it is with its works built a long ago by the Romans?"

Rom nodded.

"Well then, lying here, more dead than alive, I saw that day plain inside my head as if it were here and now. There was I, strutting like a young cock, going about and about selling my tickets and being lucky beyond my desserts, I can tell you. It seemed everyone in the whole place would see that play. I mind that, by the noonstead, I'd not a ticket left, for even the gentry from the big houses round about had sent their menservants and their maidservants to buy my wares. Now, Rom," he added hastily, sensing some of Rom's tension and misunderstanding it, "you're not to think I've remembered any single person who bought from me, nor indeed anything at all about your particular ticket. Nor am I like to, seeing that one ticket is twin to all the others."

Rom relaxed a little. Maybe it was not going to begin again. He thought he could not have borne it if Pat's memory had pointed to a fellow member of the Hallam Company.

"But here's a strange thing. And it may be of some help to you, Rom. Memory plays strange tricks, and thinking of that bit of paper a face came into my mind and hung there

142

as clear as if it were truly before my eyes. It was a face set against the streets of Bath: a good face, strong and kind and wise. And—" he paused, looking at Rom, and the pause lengthened in the quiet room until Rom thought he must cry out and did not because just in time Patrick went on. "And I've seen that very face again. Here in Williamsburg at some time within these last three months. Not a young face now—or not so young as it was then—but still as strong and kind and wise."

"Who—who is it, Pat?"

Pat's eyes were comical in their look of frustration. "I don't know, Rom. I couldn't put a name to that face then and I can't now. I only know I've seen here the very man I saw those years ago in Bath. Seen him but once, so it's not likely he spends all his time in the town. I know I saw him once before and I know it was in Bath. But that's all. And"—he held up a bandaged hand, cautioning Rom against hope—"and remember, lad, there's nothing to say this—this reappearing face goes with your ticket. There's but the one thing. If I see that man again and talk to him he might just have heard of some person living in or near Bath ten years gone who had, later, lost two children. For the one thing I'm sure is that whoever had that ticket you showed me must have been in Bath in the year 1742."

He had been sitting forward while he talked and now, as if the effort had tired him, he leaned carefully back and sighed and closed his eyes. "I'm sorry it's not more, Rom," he said, and did not see the relief in Rom's face.

There was little in this to worry about, Rom was thinking. A face twice seen, once in Bath, once again ten years and three thousand miles away, and maybe not to be seen a third time for another ten years. He leaned over Pat and put his hand gently on the bandaged arm. "You're not to worry, Pat," he said, "all will come right in good time if the Lord wills it. Now do you rest and forget me and my problems."

Patrick did not answer and Rom, looking more closely

at him, saw he was asleep and tiptoed from the room.

He did not tell Barney and Polly what he had learned. The more he thought about Pat's reappearing face the less important it seemed to him and he pushed it back into his mind, glad to forget it and with it the misery he'd known while he waited for what Pat would say. He wanted nothing to disturb the even, quiet running of the days. They were doing well now: he and Polly at the Theater, Barney happy in his work at the Printing Office.

For the first day or two Barney had come home each night drooping with tiredness, but by the third day he had found his second wind and since then he seemed as tireless as he had been when he was ropedancing. He grumbled a little on damp days but they had not come often this autumn and early winter and Barney swore that even if he was an old hop-hop it made no difference.

He brought home each night snippets of news he picked up in the shop and it was thus that Rom and Polly learned first of the reward posted for information about the men who had attacked Patrick. Everybody in the Company hoped the reward would bring some word of the attacker but when a week went by without result they began to give up their hopes. They knew only that Wynell and Herbert could have had no part in the beating for they were heard of in Maryland as members of a group of players and it was clear the two deserters could not have been in Williamsburg when Pat was hurt. Rom silently asked their pardon for suspecting them. Likely the beating had been done by some crazy persons who thought all players were sinful folk.

On the morning of December 14, Rom and Polly took the Little People from their box. The day was a Tuesday and Polly would not be needed at the Playhouse until the afternoon. Nor, since there was no bit of a part for him in that week's plays, would Rom. Since he had become a real member of the Company he had given up altogether dealing with the candles. He had got one of the Struthers boys to take his place as the other snuffles, and Old Hallam was pleased with this arrangement, as was the Struthers boy. So today seemed a good time to go over the puppets and their gear in preparation for a surprise performance for the Company during the Christmas season.

Rom was testing the rods that controlled the movements of the puppets and Polly was checking their costumes and other accessories. They had been working quietly, not talking or needing to talk, each knowing the other to be content. So Rom jumped and nearly dropped the small wrench he had just picked up, when Polly asked, "Why would anyone paint a horse, Rom?"

"A horse? You mean a toy horse or a real one?"

"A real live one."

Rom laughed. "If this is a riddle, Pol, I give it up right now."

"No, Rom. I'm not trying to catch you. I mean it."

"I still give up. There just isn't any reason to paint a horse I can think of. And it would be a deal of trouble besides. What is all this about, Pol?"

Polly smoothed the king's robe, running her fingers lovingly over the Ankh. "It's that Rafe Bascomb, Rom. I heard him yesterday when I was working alone at the Playhouse. He and another down-at-heels sort of person—I saw him when I peeped through the door to find out what they were up to—were whispering together. Rafe forgot and raised his voice and said loudly, 'I tell you we will *paint* the wretched horse and . . .' and the other hushed him and I didn't hear anything else."

"Well you must have misheard, Pol. No doubt he said house, not horse, though why Rafe Bascomb, who never does a stroke of work he doesn't have to, would be painting a house, I don't know. Not that the shack he shares with that uncle of his wouldn't be the better for some paint."

"Whatever he meant I doubt he's up to any good," Polly said, and Rom agreed, and they both forgot Rafe in making lists of what the Little People needed—a new wig for one, a bit of lace for another, colors for freshening the paint on a third.

"Can you manage to get all these, Pol?" Rom asked. "I'm supposed to spend the afternoon with Pat. He's going to give me lessons in acting every day until he's well enough to come back to the Company."

"Oh, Rom, I'm glad. Why didn't you tell me? It's a fair miracle how you've come along here in Williamsburg, where everything started so miserably. We *are* lucky, Rom."

"Yes," Rom said, and for a moment remembered the letter from their real father and felt it as a dark cloud in his mind and shook his head to send the cloud away, and took his coat from the peg. "Let's be going, then."

"I'll just run up with you to Pat's room for a minute and speak to him before I go on the errands. I've plenty of time before I'm to join Mrs. Adcock at the Playhouse."

"Pat will like that. He was asking after you yesterday."

Pat was a good teacher, patient and thorough. When Polly had talked with him a few minutes, giving him the gossip of the Playhouse, and left, he began to instruct Rom in the rules of acting.

"Now, lad, first you must learn the dramatic passions and how to show them. There are some seventy of them from Absence-of-Mind to Worrying and each has its own rules of look and gesture. Do you take Anger to begin. What will you need to show the folk in the pit you're full of wrath? A voice strong, swift and often interrupted by swells of indignation, and a fiery look to the eyes. You must speak rapidly and harshly. You must thrust out your neck and shake your head. You must draw your eyebrows together and roll your eyes one minute and stare from them the next, flare your nostrils, wrinkle your forehead, strain your muscles, and breathe audibly and fast. Open your mouth, grind your teeth together, stamp your feet, clench your fists and threaten . . ."

Rom had been trying to carry out each instruction as

146

Pat spoke it with the result he gave the impression of a contortionist at a fair trying to tie his legs about his neck. Pat tried to keep his face straight, but in the end, he was laughing too hard to finish his sentence.

Rom said in a small, hopeless voice, "Oh, Pat! I'll *never* learn."

"That you will entirely, Rom," Pat said, sobering before Rom's dismay. "Anger's the worst of the lot for complication. I was only giving you some notion of the passions. Now we'll begin again with something a bit easier."

They worked throughout the rest of the day and when dusk closed in and it was time to light the candles and build up the fire, Rom knew he had begun to understand the rules of acting. He knew, too, it would be a long time before he could master them all and he was grateful to Pat for teaching him.

"You'll do, Rom," Pat said. "In fact I'm fair proud of you, the way you've caught on. You'll make a fine actor one day and that not so far off. Now here's a word in your ear. These passions are all very fine, and sure you'll want to learn them well. But there are some in London Town— and their number's increasing each year—hold with a new way of acting, a more natural way. So do you never forget to watch men when they show anger or hurt or pity or the rest and do you bear in mind how each expresses his feeling."

Rom nodded slowly, remembering Pat's own acting. "Yes," he said. "I think you yourself hold with these men in London, Pat."

"That I do, Rom, for I've known the great Mackay himself and known him well in my time and he's the leader of this new thinking. But mind you, Rom Hormsby, no shirking the old rules. Unlearning them will come easy enough later on when you know how to handle your body and your voice. And now be off with you or Mistress Polly will think I've worked you to death entirely."

Rom started early next morning for the Playhouse. He

knew no one would be there as yet and he wanted to test yesterday's lessons on the stage, where there was more room to move about. The first snow of the year had fallen during the night and the town was a picture under its soft cover. The streets were empty and so quiet it seemed the snow had put a spell of silence upon all the normal, small sounds of the day.

Rom was halfway to the Playhouse when a burly man, his face, except for his eyes, hidden between the turned-up collar of his greatcoat and the pulled-down point of his tricorne hat, loomed before him as if he had grown suddenly straight up out of the ground.

"Romulus Hormsby?" he asked in a voice more than half muffled by the collar.

"I am," Rom said, and looked closely at the man and recognized him as the town constable, and added, "as you very well know, Jared Strunk."

"That's as may be," Jared Strunk said. "Do you come along, Romulus Hormsby, and no back talk either, do you understand?" He seized Rom's arm and tried to pull him away from the Playhouse.

"Come along? Come along where? Leave go of my arm, Jared. I'm in no mood for japing and have no time for it." He tried to jerk away from the constable but Jared Strunk only held him more firmly.

"No jape as you well know, young Hormsby, though I'd as well say straight out I'd not have thought it of you."

"Thought what of me?" Rom tried again to twist away from him. "What are you talking about?"

"You'll not be needing me to tell you, young villain. You can ask Jailer when you're proper locked up, if you like."

"Jailer? Locked up?" Rom felt bewildered and trapped and, suddenly, afraid.

"Will you come along peaceful, Romulus Hormsby, or must I tie up your hands and drag you at rope's end?"

Rom's thoughts swirled about like fog in his mind. What was this about? And, more important, what should he do?

Jared Strunk must have lost his wits. He might even turn violent, like the poor mad creatures in Bedlam in London, if he were crossed. Best humor him until they came to the jail. There'd be help there from the jailer. "Very well," Rom said, "let us go. But do, please, loose my arm. You're hurting me."

"Isn't that just a pity and a shame," Jared Strunk said in a nasty voice, and tightened his hold until Rom would have cried out with pain if he had not, for pride, shut his teeth hard and kept back the sound.

Neither of them spoke again as they went past the Capitol, empty and still in the early day, and down the white covered hillside to the neat, brick jailhouse. They saw nobody and Rom was glad for he felt it shameful to be hauled along thus like a criminal even if it were only because of the whim of a madman.

The jail was almost as cold as it had been outside. The jailer sat at a great desk writing in a ledger and he did not look up when Jared Strunk pushed Rom roughly into the room. Rom waited a moment, but he had no stomach for patience or politeness and when the jailer paid no attention he shouted, "Tell this—this lunatic to let me go! This is an . . ."

Jared Strunk took careful aim with his free hand and struck Rom's mouth. The sound was loud above the scratching of the quill pen and the jailer said, "That will do, Strunk. I'll have no prisoner mistreated, not even a horse thief."

"Horse thief!" Rom could only whisper the words through lips that ached and stung from Jared's slap. "What—what are you saying? I am no horse thief."

The jailer looked up then and saw Jared Strunk raising his hand again and spoke sharply, "I *said* that will do. Be off with you, Strunk. Leave the boy to me."

"Leave you alone with him? Not likely. He do be a vicious young brute."

"Well, he's not marked you at any rate, Strunk. You heard me. Now be off."

The constable glared at Rom as if he would like to beat him, but after a moment he left the room. Rom rubbed the aching spot above his elbow and winced as the blood began to flow into it once more.

The jailer said, "Well. What have you to say for yourself?"

Rom licked his lips and coughed. His throat felt constricted, as if he were choking on a fish bone. He did not recognize as his own the voice that came from him. "You —you accuse *me* of stealing a horse?"

"Not I," the jailer said. "I accuse no one. Colonel Littleton accuses you."

"Colonel Littleton! But I've never even seen the man."

The jailer turned to his desk and read from the ledger on it, "'Upon information received, I, Robert Littleton, Councilor, do accuse one Romulus Hormsby of the theft of my bay horse Remus and do demand that the said Romulus Hormsby be taken into custody and held for trial at the Court of Oyer and Terminer.' What say you to that, boy?"

"Remus," Rom said. "I'm accused of stealing *Remus?* But how? And why? And when?"

"Do you deny you stole the horse?"

Rom found full voice. "Deny it! Of course I deny it. I take my solemn oath upon all I hold most sacred I did not steal Remus, nor have I seen him since the day of the race."

He could not believe this was happening to him. He knew he should do something to free himself from the charge. But he couldn't think what. Horse thief! The penalty for stealing a horse was—*hanging.* And the jailer didn't believe he was innocent. The jailer was writing again in the ledger, not even bothering to ask further questions.

"Councilor Littleton accuses. Romulus Hormsby denies. Romulus Hormsby to be held in custody until . . ."

"*No!*" Rom shouted. "No! You cannot do this. I did not steal—. When? *When* was Remus stolen?"

"Yesterday afternoon between three and four of the clock."

"Then it *could* not have been I." Rom felt as if an enormous weight had been taken away from his chest. "Between three and four of the clock yesterday afternoon I was in the company of Patrick Malone. I could not have been stealing a horse."

The jailer laughed disagreeably. "Does not everyone know that Patrick Malone lies near to death from the beating he took in the Playhouse? Do you think to make sport of me, boy?"

Rom beat his hands upon the desk. "He is *not* near to death. He is mending, and he is teaching me the rules of acting the while and I *was* there yesterday from two of the clock onwards."

"A likely story, indeed. We'll cool you off in the cells quick enough," the jailer said, and stretched a hand toward a bell beside him.

"Wait!" Rom was frantic. "Do you send for Mr. Lewis Hallam. He will be witness for me."

"What has Mr. Lewis Hallam to do with the likes of you?" the jailer asked, but he did not ring the bell.

"I'm a member of his Company."

"You! Are you mad, boy, that you expect me to believe such a tale? We're none so deaf in the jailhouse we've not heard the story of Barnabas Hormsby and his brats. Snuffles you may be, but no member of the Company of Comedians. Send for Mr. Hallam on behalf of his candle snuffer! Not likely!"

"I *am* a member of his Company. I *am*. When Patrick Malone was sorely hurt and Mr. Wynell and Mr. Herbert left, Mr. Hallam signed me on. He did. He did. And he's having me taught by Mr. Patrick Malone. Send for him. Send for Mr. Hallam. Ask him." Rom was almost sobbing in his earnestness.

The jailer looked at him, less sure now that the boy was lying. He was not a quick-witted man, though honest and prepared to be kind. He wondered if the boy would keep on in this way if there were not some truth in what he said. Maybe it would be wise to pay some attention to him. He pulled at his ear, pondering, and Rom, seeing him uncertain, guessing he was weakening, made one more pleading try.

"Would I be urging you to send for Mr. Hallam if I were not telling the truth? Would I be anxious to see him if I did not believe he can help me and will? Would I lie about him when a lie can be so easily proven?"

The jailer stopped pulling his ear and nodded slowly. "There do be some little sense in that," he said, and slammed the desk top shut and locked it and went to a door that led out of the room and called, "Samuel! You Samuel! Do you run quick to Mr. Lewis Hallam and ask if he'll step round to the jailhouse soon as might be convenient on behalf of Romulus Hormsby."

CHAPTER FOURTEEN

"You'd as well sit," the jailer said when a clatter of feet on the stairs beyond the door had told them the unseen Samuel was on his way. "I've no mind to put you in irons below, long as there be any question you might, of truth, be innocent. You're over young for sharing the cells with murderers. But do you keep a still tongue in your head, for I've work to do and I'll not have you pestering me with your nattering."

Rom sat on a stool in the corner and waited. The town must be full awake now. Somewhere nearby a man was singing sadly to himself an old riddle song:

"I gave my love a cherry that had no stone.
I gave my love a chicken that had no bone.
I gave my love a ring that had no end.
And I gave my love a baby with no cryen."

The singer went away or tired of the song, but the melody kept going round in Rom's head as accompaniment to his disconnected thoughts.

Why didn't Old Hallam come?

What would Barney and Polly think?

How could anyone think he'd steal a horse—any horse, let alone Remus?

How long had it been since Samuel left?

He beat his forehead with the heel of his hand and the jailer looked round at the soft thuds and glared at him and he stopped. The jailer's pen scratched, and snow, beginning to fall again, whispered against the small glass panes in the window. Rom got up and started to walk back and forth across the end of the room and the jailer barked at him, "Sit down or I *will* put the irons on you."

Rom started to protest, and the door behind him opened quietly and Old Hallam said, "What's going on? What's wrong with you, Romulus? I came along at top speed, thinking you hurt or in some ill-taking, and now I find you hale and sound. Well, speak up. Speak up, one of you."

"So," the jailer said slowly, "you do know the lad."

"Know him! Of course I know him. He's Romulus Hormsby, once my candle snuffer, now a member of my Company, who's supposed to be spending his time learning the business of acting, not kicking his heels in jailhouses."

"He's kicking his heels by my sufferance, if you please. By rights they should be fast held by ankle irons in the cells below. Yon innocent-looking boy's accused of horse stealing and like to pay with his life if he can't prove different. He claims you'll be a witness for him."

Lewis Hallam's face was red with anger. "What scoundrel makes such false accusation? What scoundrel?"

154

"I'd not thought to hear any man name Colonel Robert Littleton scoundrel," the jailer said dryly, holding out the ledger to Hallam.

"Bob—Littleton?" Hallam's face turned from red to white as he skimmed the writing. "Upon information received," he repeated to himself. "What information? Whose information? Who dares . . . ?"

"That I couldn't say. An accusation's been made. It's not my business to question it. My business is to keep this jail and the prisoners in it."

Hallam put the ledger on a small, rough table near him and went to Rom and put an arm about his shoulders. "What say you to this, Romulus?" he asked gently.

"That there's no word of truth in it, sir. The jailer says Remus was stolen between three and four of the clock, yesterday afternoon. I was then, and for an hour before and an hour after, with Patrick Malone, learning somewhat of the dramatic passions as you bade me do."

"Yes. That I can vouch, for Patrick told me of your studies when I spoke to him last night."

The jailer broke in, looking startled, "But all men know Patrick Malone's near to death from a beating," he said, a little angrily.

"Then all men know a lie as you can see for yourself do you care to step round to Daniel Fisher's tenement," Lewis Hallam replied, without taking his eyes from Rom's face. "Before two of the clock, Rom, where were you?"

"With Polly at the Widow Dawson's, as the Widow herself will tell you, for we begged the use of her common room and she was herself in and out the whole morning and saw us there."

"Good. And thereafter?"

"Polly was with me until we got to Pat's room, and after she left I stayed with him till nightfall. Then I went home and—and"—he had suddenly remembered and he finished triumphantly—"I met Papa and another of the

155

printers outside the door of the Ordinary and we walked together all the way to the Widow Dawson's."

Hallam turned to the jailer. "You hear him, keeper. The full day accounted for and a witness for each hour. How could he steal a horse? Release the lad at once."

The jailer shook his head stolidly. "Not I," he said, and pointed to the ledger. "Innocent he may be and that do seem a sure thing, but I'll not let him go without Colonel Littleton bids me do so."

"Come, man," Hallam yelled at him. "Do you think Bob Littleton would have you hold him one minute longer than it takes to prove him innocent? Release him, I say, and get your authorization later. I'll be responsible to Colonel Littleton."

The jailer shook his head again. "That I'll not do, Mr. Lewis Hallam. With respect, sir, you are little more than a stranger here, a stranger new come among us. I'll take my orders from Colonel Littleton and from no one else."

Hallam, his hands curling and uncurling at his sides, took a step toward the jailer and stopped. He wanted to shake the slow-speaking, bullheaded man more than he'd ever wanted anything else. But he guessed it would cause trouble for himself and do no good for Rom's cause. "Very well," he said, "I will, myself, go at once and fetch Colonel Littleton's written release. Do you have patience, Rom. We'll have you out of here before another hour's gone. And you, keeper, if you lay a finger on this boy while I'm gone I'll have your job!"

They had, however, more than twice an hour to wait. Each minute lagged after the next and the time would have seemed closer to two days had not the jailer at last taken pity on Rom's restlessness and brought out of his desk a square of leather scored with lines and numbers and bade him sit and play a game of Nine Men's Morris. Rom gave his whole attention to the game and placed each of the nine bits of red leather that were his men, one after the other upon the board and moved them cannily until he had three in a row and could take one of the jailer's pieces. In a few minutes he was so absorbed in playing he forgot time and looked up in surprise when a knock at the door was followed at once by the entrance of Lewis Hallam and a tall, handsomely dressed gentleman with thick white hair, though he was, Rom judged, no older than Old Hallam.

"Here's your Colonel Littleton come himself to talk to your prisoner," Old Hallam said, and Rom thought with a catch of fear that he was not at ease about the Colonel's presence.

The jailer had jumped to his feet, almost knocking over the table in his hurry to show proper respect to the newcomer. He started at once to speak, but Littleton held up his hand and the jailer was, abruptly, silent. The Colonel had not stopped looking at Rom from the time he had followed Hallam through the door. His eyes were deepset and their look seemed to go straight through Rom and Rom fidgeted, feeling uncomfortable under the stare.

"Have I your permission to question this lad, Lewis?" the Colonel asked, at last.

"Why else did you come with me, Bob?" Lewis Hallam said in a restrained kind of voice. He went on, to Rom, in explanation, "Colonel Littleton would have your story from your own lips, not being, apparently, willing to take my word."

The jailer looked smug. Rom stiffened his back and glared at Colonel Littleton and started to speak. The Colonel gave him no time. "Now, Romulus Hormsby, do you hear me first," he said. "Late last night my man Enoch Brown came to me in my office. He was distressed and seemed unwilling to say what he knew he must say. He told me a—a person who would not give his name nor let himself be clearly seen had come to the stable at dusk and told a tale of having seen 'the one who rode Remus on race day'—you, I believe, Romulus Hormsby—leading the horse by stealth along a forest path at four of the clock.

Before Enoch Brown could question him, the informer took to his heels and disappeared into the ending day. Enoch went at once to Remus's stall and found him gone indeed, and spent an hour searching for him without result and came, at last, to me. Remus is a valuable animal, and when I was sure he was truly gone I lodged a complaint against you. Your friend, Lewis Hallam, believes you innocent but—you look an intelligent boy—you must see I'd want to hear your story for myself."

Rom was tired and irritated. He could, in fact, see no reason why this Colonel Littleton wanted to hear the whole tale again from the beginning, but he knew it would likely do no more than waste time if he delayed in telling it. So, step by step, he repeated what he had told the jailer and Old Hallam.

The Colonel listened without interrupting and, when Rom had done, walked to the window and stood looking out. The eerie snowlight fell full upon his profile and for a moment Rom had an impression he knew this man. Then Littleton turned away and the impression faded.

"Will this man Malone confirm this story, Lewis?" Littleton asked.

"Of a certainty." Hallam's voice was testy. "Would you hear it from his own lips, Bob, since you seem loathe to take my word?"

"No, no," Littleton said quickly. "If you assure me he will confirm, it is enough."

"I do assure you. For the third time."

"Bear with me, Lewis. I am fair out of my mind with worry over Remus." He turned to the jailer. "Release the boy and destroy the complaint." He rubbed his forehead as if his head ached, then held out his hand to Rom. "I can but ask your pardon, Romulus Hormsby. If I can ever serve you I am yours to command. In the meantime I shall try to seek out your accuser and see he is punished for laying a false information against you. *If* I can find him. Thank you, Lewis, for setting all straight."

He went abruptly to the door and through it, leaving them with no further word of good-by.

"Poor Bob," Hallam said softly. "He's had many heavy sorrows in his life and he loves that horse. Do you not bear him malice, Rom."

Rom shook his head. He would bear no malice. Something about the look of Colonel Littleton as he had left them had been so lost, so unhappy, Rom had found his irritation and near anger turning to pity and wished he could find Remus and return him.

It was not until the next day that Rom had a chance to tell Polly about his experience. She had already gone to the Playhouse when, after a long afternoon's work at his lessons, he came to the Widow Dawson's. Barney, the Widow Dawson told him, was at the Raleigh, and after a supper of bread and cheese Rom had gone at once to sleep.

He had been too tired to think about Remus as he readied himself for bed, but he awoke next morning with the certainty that Rafe Bascomb had been his accuser— or had been, at least, responsible for the accusation. Rafe would not know about the lessons with Pat for no one knew except Polly and Old Hallam. Rafe would believe Rom could not prove his innocence. Rafe was the only person in all Williamsburg who would want to do Rom any harm, unless it were young Lewis making mischief for the very devil of it and this plot was too subtle for young Lewis.

Rafe it had to be. And, lying in his bed sleepily, thinking of Rafe, Rom remembered the curious bit of overheard talk about painting a horse. Suddenly he was no longer sleepy. What exactly had Polly said? He couldn't remember, and he fell all over himself getting out of bed and dressed for the day.

Within five minutes he was knocking upon Polly's door and calling her to hurry with her own dressing. While he waited for her he walked back and forth in the short third-floor hall, nearly forgetting each turn to duck his head so he would not bang it upon the ceiling that slanted steeply under the roof. When Polly came, looking starched and crisp and wide-awake, though she, too, had hurried, he sprang at once into questions about what she had overheard.

She took a minute, frowning, to be sure she quoted correctly before she repeated, "'I tell you we will *paint* the wretched horse.'"

"Was that all, Pol? Are you quite sure you've remembered every single word?"

"Yes. Quite sure, Rom. The other man hushed Rafe at once, and what else they may have said was spoken in whispers, too softly for me to hear. Why, Rom? Why are you so suddenly curious about all this? I thought you . . ."

"That was the day before yesterday," he interrupted. "Come along. I'm fair starved, having had but little supper last night, and I've no mind to eat cold cornbread. We'll go to Mr. Wetherburn's tavern and have a proper breakfast and I'll tell you."

They walked the block to the inn, single file, picking their way through runnels of water from melting snow. It was not until they were in a quiet corner of one of the inner rooms with their plates before them that Rom told her all that had happened to him upon the preceding day.

"Poor Colonel Littleton," Polly said when he had done and she had expressed proper horror and concern for his grim experience. "It would be a direful thing truly to have such a horse and lose him. Oh, Rom, I wish *we* could find Remus."

"That's what we're going to do." Rom spoke slowly as if he were pondering something he did not quite understand. "There is something—something about Colonel Littleton tugs at you. Tugs and makes you want to—to be his man as a knight in olden times was man to his liege lord. It's something—I think it is something about his eyes which are or—or seem to be—ocean deep in sadness. Even when

I was—was angered because he did not, at first, believe me and made me tell my story over again to him, even then I—I wanted to serve him. And I can think of no better thing we could do than find Remus for him."

"Yes, Rom. But saying's easier than doing. How can we even go *about* finding him? We don't know enough of this country to guess where to begin to look."

"If I'm right in what I'm thinking, Pol, we don't need to know the countryside. Now listen and see if you think I could be right?" He paused to get his thoughts clear and Polly said impatiently, "Well. Go on."

"Yes. Well, about what you heard Rafe say. If you wanted to steal a horse and—and disguise him, what would you do?"

Polly shook her head. "I've no idea."

"Change his color!" Rom prompted.

"Of course, Rom. Change his color and hide his special markings. *Paint* him!"

Rom nodded, grinning at her.

"But could you, Rom? Could you do such a thing without hurting the poor creature?"

"I think—I'm sure you could. If you used say soot—dissolved in water—and put on a thin coat, just enough to cover, you'd do no more harm to the animal than—than if you washed him in plain water."

"I believe—I do believe you're right, Rom. But—but how will that help us find Remus? Even if it's what Rafe was talking about. We still don't know where to look."

"It's not likely," Rom said slowly, thinking it out, "that Rafe stole the horse *just* to make trouble for me. Or even if that were his only aim at first, it's not likely he'd pass over the chance to sell so fine an animal. And there'd be plenty in the Colony, I'd guess, would buy the horse and take him south, to the Carolinas, or north, and no questions asked."

"So?" Polly asked.

"So, I doubt Rafe has yet had time to send Remus along.

And if we keep a close watch on Rafe Bascomb we'll see where he goes and what he does and sooner or later he'll *lead* us to Remus. He'll be bound to feed the horse with all this snow on the ground."

"Rom!" Polly sounded impressed with his reasoning. "Rom, I do believe you've got it."

"Can you leave your costumes today? We should begin watching at once because I'm sure Rafe will want to get Remus away as quickly as possible. Every day he keeps him nearby could be a danger." If they were not already too late, he thought, and would not say the thought aloud for fear of making it come true.

"Yes," Polly said, "I'm sure it will be all right. Everything's ready for tomorrow night. But I'll have to tell Mrs. Adcock. And what about your lessons?"

"I'll have to tell Pat, too, of course, that I'll likely not be there this afternoon. But I'm sure he won't mind if I explain why. Come on. Let's hurry to the tenement. They will both be there now."

CHAPTER FIFTEEN

The back of Rom's neck ached from holding his muscles tight against making an unexpected noise. He wanted to sneeze and pressed a finger sidewise against his nose until the fit passed. Beside him, Polly waited as still as he, and neither looked away from the door of the tumble-down hut they had been watching for upward of three hours.

When they had first come here to the edge of the forest Rom had crept on his hands and knees to the single, dirt-caked window and stealthily raised himself until he could see through the one small clear space which someone had wiped clean for a spyhole. He had stayed just long enough to make sure Rafe was inside and crept back to Polly, hidden already in the thicket of scarlet-berried holly. Here they had waited, tense and watchful, while the hours passed and the forest whispered and creaked with the slow sound of thaw and they were grateful the weather had turned warm after the snow.

A rabbit jumped from the forest and saw them and sat upon its haunches and watched them distrustfully, its nose wrinkling in uncertainty. Polly moved closer to Rom and whispered, "Look," and Rom closed his hand over her arm and hushed her, pointing toward the hut.

The door they watched was cracked open and held so, while Rafe looked out to satisfy himself there was no one about. Rom held his breath, hoping they had chosen their cover well. If Rafe saw them or sensed their presence their long wait would go for nothing and likely, with Rafe warned, they'd never find Remus.

The crack gaped wide and Rafe stood in the doorway. He stretched his arms over his head and yawned loudly. The rabbit, frightened at the ugly sound, jumped straight into the air and landed running, and Rafe, startled, stared at the place where it had been. Rom held Polly's arm hard, willing her to stillness, but he had no need. She was as aware as he of the necessity for quiet. Both of them, as if moved by a single thought, pressed closer into the thicket, unmindful of pricks from the sharp spikes of the holly leaves.

They could see Rafe's lips moving, but they could not hear what he said. After two seconds he stooped and picked up a stone and threw it toward the place where the rabbit had sat. The stone just missed hitting Polly, but she did not move or cry out, and Rafe, satisfied he was alone, moved away from the hut.

They let him get a good start before they went after him, cautiously. He was not, it seemed, in a hurry. Nor did he seem aware that his way was marked and followed for he took no precautions to hide it. He went boldly along a narrow path that led through the forest and they paced him easily, keeping under cover, moving from tree to tree, a little in his rear.

The path wound so crookedly among pines and hollies, that before Rom knew where they were, they had come upon the secret, hidden glade he had found so many weeks ago. He pulled Polly to a quick stop when he saw Rafe go close to the screen of myrtleberries and part them and peer through.

At once the quiet of the forest was torn by the shrill, high whinny of an angry horse. Polly said quietly, "Rom! You were right," and Rom nodded and answered beneath his breath, "Come on. We'll surprise him."

They left the sheltering trees and dashed across the little space that separated them from Rafe before he had time to guess at their presence.

"Good day to you, Rafe," Rom said when they had come close enough for him to touch Rafe.

Rafe looked at him stupidly. "You . . ." he said, "what do you be doing about in this place. You do be in jailhouse!"

"What do you know about that, Rafe? Was it you laid a false information to make sure I'd be taken up by the constable? And likely hung for a horse thief? How else could you know of it?"

"Think to catch me out, do you, Snuffles? I did hear it last night in the town."

"Where in the town?"

"Belike at the Raleigh. In the taproom where I'd been sent by Mr. Adcock for a pint of ale."

"That you did not. No more than four others beside myself knew the tale, and they knew me freed and clear and the charge against me destroyed before the sun was noonhigh yesterday. *You* are the horse thief, Rafe."

"You lie, Snuffles."

"Do you deny there's a horse hidden beyond the myrtleberries?"

"A wild horse is there, surely. Every man needs a horse and I went along the river and found the wild herd and caught one of them and brought it here."

Rom pretended to believe him. "That does interest me, Rafe. I've heard of the wild horses but I've not seen one.

165

I've heard too they are useless when caught, being either too old or too sick to fight."

"I did catch me a young one, Snuffles."

"Let us go together to look at him, then."

Rafe's eyes were wary. He took a step away from Rom and shook his head. "Best not," he said. "The beast, though young, is fierce and angry now at being caught. It might do you some hurt, did you go near."

"And that would fair break your sorrowing heart," Rom said, and caught Rafe and spun him about. "March! Rafe, or I'll break every bone in your sniveling nose."

Rafe tried to pull away but when he found he could in no way loose Rom's hold went, reluctantly, through the hedge. Polly came behind and drew in her breath with delight, for a moment forgetting why they were here in her pleasure at the forest room. The next moment she forgot everything except the black horse tethered to an iron stake driven into the ground.

Rom had pushed Rafe ahead of him as they came through the hedge and the horse, at first sight of him, went wild. He screamed his hatred and rage at this enemy and tore at the stake, lunging again and again toward Rafe's cringing figure. The horse had almost succeeded in pulling the stake loose when Rom stepped clear of Rafe's shielding body and said, very softly, "Remus. Quiet Remus. Quiet."

At once the horse stopped plunging and whickered a welcome. With one eye on Rafe to see he did not try to run away, Rom went close to the horse, which nuzzled his shoulder, whinnying soft greetings. Rom rubbed the black nose and said, "Polly, see if you can clean off some of this blacking."

Polly took her kerchief and dampened it in the snow still lying, in spite of the thaw, in this sheltered place and rubbed at a spot on the horse's face. The black came away easily, showing a white star against a light bay coat. She stooped to clean Remus's slim legs, but Rom did not wait

for further proof. He stood in front of Rafe, who refused
to meet his eyes.

"A wild horse is it then, Rafe? Yon animal is Remus, the
best horse in Colonel Robert Littleton's stable, as you well
know."

"I know nothing of any Remus," Rafe said sulkily. "I did come by chance upon this place but yesterday and found the horse as you see him and pitied him and brought him food and water and did return today to see if he was still here. There be no harm in that."

"And what of the horse you promised to paint, Rafe Bascomb?" Polly asked.

"What do you mean, mistress?" Rafe tried to look innocent.

"You know right well. I heard you, Rafe, when you talked with your—your fellow close by the Playhouse two days ago."

"It was my uncle I spoke with and it was—was a *house* we spoke of painting, not a horse."

Rom said, "Come then. We'll take Remus together to Colonel Littleton and tell him all you've told us here."

There was no bluster left in Rafe. His eyes were staring with fear. Strange whimpering noises came from his chattering teeth and his whole body seemed trying to shrink into itself and away from Rom.

Rom started to take his arm, but before he could do so Polly knocked against her brother and threw him, for a moment, off balance. In that moment Rafe Bascomb turned and ran, blundering through the thicket.

Rom started after him but Polly said sharply, "Let him go, Rom!" and he turned to her in anger.

"Why?" he shouted. "Why should I let him go when he's a horse thief and—and likely worse?"

"Because," Polly said, holding him by the very quietness of her purpose, "because stealing a horse is a hanging matter here. If you catch Rafe he'll surely hang. He's but a poor unfortunate, Rom. He can't help being a bully and a scoundrel. Mrs. Adcock told me something of him, only last night. He's been beaten and half-starved by his villainous uncle since his parents—decent folk enough, though poor—died of the wasting sickness when Rafe was

168

a very little boy. Could you sleep of nights if his hanging were on your head? I couldn't."

Rom was frowning at her. Why were there always so many sides to every question, he wondered. Rafe had been willing enough to send *him* to the gallows, but if what Polly had said was true—and he had no cause to question it—he surely did not wish to see Rafe hang. Hanging seemed, in any case, too dear a price to pay for stealing a horse, though no doubt there was some good cause for the law. But Rafe was a troublemaker, whatever his reasons. He should be punished somehow, taught some kind of lesson that would improve his behavior.

Polly said, "He's good and frightened now, Rom. I don't doubt he's learned his lesson and will make no more mischief for you, if indeed he dares show his face in Williamsburg again. In some other place, where he's not known and is away from his uncle, he'll likely do better. Mrs. Adcock says he's been talking of taking the King's shilling and joining the crew of one of the fighting sloops on the Virginia Station in the river. Would that not be better than getting him hung, Rom?"

Rom nodded slowly.

"And will you keep silence about Remus?" she went on, "or at least about Rafe's part in stealing him?"

"How can I, Pol? We must give some explanation to Enoch Brown." Rom had gone back to the horse and unleashed him from the stake and stood beside him, rubbing the white star gently.

"You can say we found him by chance and guessed him to be Remus when he seemed to know you, and knew he was when you rubbed his nose and the blacking came off and showed the white star."

"Ouch!" Rom said as Remus nibbled his ear affectionately. "My ear's my own, old horse, and not for your eating. We'll take you home to Enoch now and he'll give you oats instead." He slipped Remus's halter over his head and took it in one hand and held out the other to Polly. "Come,

Pol, and let your mind rest easy. I'll not name Rafe Bascomb."

After all, he thought, he did owe Rafe something, even if it was a sort of left-handed owing, for it was through Rafe he'd been freed of his own stupid cowardice. "But," he added fiercely to Polly, "if I ever set eyes on his ugly face again, I'll give him the thorough thrashing he's been asking for."

Polly grinned up at him and her eyes shone with mischief, but she held her peace as they started, leading Remus, for Colonel Littleton's house.

CHAPTER SIXTEEN

"Master Rom! Master Rom! Master Rom!"

Rom finally heard the soft, persistent call and came sluggishly back from his study of a scene in Mr. Addison's *Cato* which Pat had set him to learn.

"Master Rom! Master Rom! Do you be within?"

Rom went to the little window set in the roof that sloped steeply in his attic room and tugged it open, holding it wide with one hand while he thrust his head out into the still, cold air. The small boy who stood on the cobbles below was familiar. He had been helping Enoch Brown with the horses at the Littleton house when Rom and Polly had taken Remus home yesterday. Rom grinned to himself, remembering Enoch Brown's surprise and joy when they had called him to come out and shown him Remus and told the tale they had agreed upon. Enoch had been sure Colonel Littleton himself would want to thank them, perhaps give them a reward, and he had bade them wait while he saw to Remus's care. But Rom and Polly, each knowing without the need for words that the other wanted neither reward nor thanks, had gone quickly home as soon as Enoch's back was turned.

"What's amiss, Amos?" Rom called down to the boy.

"The Colonel say do you kindly favor him by coming to the house," Amos said.

The devil take the Colonel, Rom thought. Would he never be done with thanks he didn't want?

"Give my compliments to the Colonel, Amos," he said, "and beg him to excuse me today for I must be about my studies."

The small face crumpled into worry. "Now, Master Rom," Amos wailed, "you not going to bid me take any such of a message to the Colonel! Colonel'll whip me sure, do I come back without you."

Rom shifted his hands upon the window sash. "Shame on you, Amos. You know Colonel Littleton would never whip you."

"No sir, Master Rom. That do be the truth. But he'll do—do *something*. He won't like it. He told me to bring you and what the Colonel tell me do, I'm going to *do*. I'm going to stand right here and I'm going to keep on hollering at you till you come, Master Rom."

Rom sighed. Amos meant what he said. He'd as well go and get it over with. "All right, Amos," he said, "I'll come," and took his head out of the window and eased the sash closed and got his coat.

Ten minutes later Amos pushed open the white front door of the Littleton house and, with a courteous deep bow that looked somehow absurd in so small a boy, ushered Rom into a quiet, gracious room. "I'll just tell Colonel you be come, Master Rom. Do you make yourself to home," Amos said, and bowed again and left.

Rom thought he had never seen so fine a place. The walls of this room, covered in a soft rose-figured damask, took the fire's light until they glowed. Ceiling-high book-shelves flanked each side of the wide chimney piece and were balanced across the room by glass-enclosed shelves which held gleaming silver pieces and other figures Rom could not quite make out from where he stood beside the door.

He waited, not knowing whether it would be proper for him to examine the cases more closely, expecting each moment to hear Colonel Littleton coming. When the Colonel did not come, Rom's curiosity grew until he could no longer contain it and he went across the room to one of the cases which stood, shadowed, in a corner.

The case held several beautifully made puppets. Rom stared at them, wishing they were in full light, wishing there were no panes of glass between him and the figures. They looked remarkably like his own Little People, but he could not be sure. He would ask Colonel Littleton about them. It might be, if these were like the Hormsby Puppets, the Colonel could tell him more of theirs, something of where they came from and who made them.

He turned away, impatient now for the coming of his host, and the skirt of his coat caught a book lying upon a low table and knocked it to the floor. He stooped to replace it, guilty at his clumsiness. The leather binding was soft and smooth and he passed his hand over it, savoring the feel of it. His fingers told him there was tooling on the side held away from him and he turned it over and almost dropped it again.

There, pressed in gold upon the dark red leather, was the Ankh, the same symbol of life so familiar to him from his own Puppet King's royal robe.

He placed the book slowly and carefully on the table. His hands moved mechanically for his mind was not upon what he was doing.

Puppets like his own.

The Ankh stamped in gold upon a book.

A face half-recognized in snowlight from the jailhouse

window: half-recognized, he now knew, because it was
so like the face of his own Puppet King.

What was the meaning of all these things? They could not all be coincidence. He was sure, yet could give no reason for the assurance, they all went together, or would if he could only find the key. He stood quite still, except for the first finger of his right hand which traced the outlines of the cross of life upon the book and slowly, up from the deeps of his mind, another memory came.

He was no longer in the quiet library of a house in Williamsburg, Colony of Virginia, nor was the time the year 1752. He was back in England, in a wide room, in a place he could not name. He was only a small lump beneath the coverings in the curtained depths of the big bed, for he was a very little boy. He was just waking out of a dream that was sweet and as familiar to him as his own hand, for it came often in his sleep. He lay, savoring the dream, thinking of the warmth and comfort it always brought him. It was a simple dream and short. In it a tall man with deep, clear eyes and thick, black hair leaned above him. Beside the man, a lady dressed in a white gown with silver trimmings that sparkled, her hair as fair as the man's was dark, bent over the small boy and called him her sweeting and kissed him. And the dream ended.

And as it ended two faces came clearly side by side into Rom's mind—the face of the man in the dream and the carved, wooden face of the Puppet King, and they were the same face. Then, another face moved into place beside them. It was, again, the same in its shape and in all its main features and it was the face of Colonel Littleton as he stood beside the window in the jailhouse.

Rom lifted the book from the table and looked again at the gold tooling. It wavered before his eyes and he knew his hands were shaking, as his spirit was shaken and rent once more with anger and hate.

He had found his father. He was sure of it. And he hated the instinct that made him sure. Colonel Littleton—the unnatural father who had written the order that sent his own children to abandonment, to—murder?

Rom turned toward the door, still holding the book, conscious only that he must get out of this room and this house before Colonel Littleton—before his father—came. His hand was reaching for the doorknob when it turned and the door was pulled outward and Colonel Littleton stood in the hall, his white hair touched to gold by sunlight from the window behind him.

"I do give you thanks, Romulus Hormsby," he began at once and formally, and broke off and looked at Rom and spoke again, quickly, "What is it, Romulus? Are you ill? Your face is white as—as death itself and you are shaking. Did you take an ague searching for Remus? Come, sit down."

He put out his hand as if he would steady Rom, and Rom jerked away from it.

"Do you not touch me," Rom said and held out the book and pointed to the Ankh. "What—what is that?"

Colonel Littleton looked at the sign and, again, at Rom's face, and wondered if the boy had lost his wits. What was there in the tooling on a book to put him into such a state? He spoke slowly and reasonably, hoping to quiet Rom by humoring him. "It's an Ankh, Romulus. It is a symbol of life and was dear to my ancestor when he was one of the greatest of all puppet makers a long time ago in Italy. His son brought the puppets to England and prospered." He wondered why he was talking on like this, but the boy's eyes were getting wilder rather than quieter and the Colonel continued. "The Ankh has become a kind of emblem to our house, an emblem we're proud of and . . ."

His voice trailed off in puzzlement as he watched Rom standing white and rigid before him. There was a look of loathing in the boy's eyes the Colonel could not understand. He tried once more to reach through this hostility and arouse some kinder response in Romulus Hormsby.

"The puppets, all that is left of them for some are lost, are there if you . . ."

Rom had found his voice and it lashed across the space between them, like a snake striking to unleash its venom. He had little notion of what words he said, knowing only the need to say something to hurt the man before him.

Colonel Littleton's face flushed, and anger reached out to Rom's hatred, but before he could speak Rom went on. "You—vile—cruel—beast of a man. How can you smile so smoothly and prate of ancestors and pride of house when you . . ." he choked on his own wrath and swallowed and went on, "when you ordered your own son and daughter abandoned—to their death, for all you knew or cared."

Colonel Littleton reached out and took hold of Rom and shook him hard. "What are you saying, boy? What do you know of all this?" he asked, and his face was as white as Rom's.

Rom tried to speak and could not, for his breath was shaken out of him, and Colonel Littleton took his hands away and shouted, "Speak, I tell you. What do you know of my son and my daughter? How . . . ?"

Rom took a deep breath and raised his own voice until it topped the Colonel's. "Never *mind!* Answer my question. Tell me true why you gave orders they be—be got rid of!"

He was so bent upon getting an answer he had no mind for anything else and he did not know their shouting had gone beyond the room and aroused the household and alarmed it, until a quiet, firm voice cut beneath the sound of anger. "What is this, Bob? What is the trouble between the two of you that you brawl like drunken sailors and shake the whole house with your angry words? I will not have it, do you hear? I will not have it in this house!"

Rom heard the words and, beyond the words, the quality of the voice, and his eyes snapped away from Colonel Littleton and his fingers, which had been curling into fists, relaxed, for the voice was the voice of the lady in his

176

dream, clouded now with irritation. He stared at the
woman in the doorway and her face was the face of the
dream lady, or like it, though it was sad and lined with
time and worry. He rubbed his hands across his eyes, trying to still the pounding that made his head ache, but it
did no good."

". . . some knowledge of our dear lost ones," he half-
heard Colonel Littleton saying. "But he will tell me nothing unless I answer his foolish and impertinent questions."

The lady crossed to Colonel Littleton. Her voice was
low, now, and calm. "Then answer him, Bob. Whatever"
—for a moment the steady voice broke—"whatever is needful to release what he knows to us, do you do it and
quickly. I—I cannot—cannot bear . . ."

She faltered once more and this time she did not go on
but hid her face against Colonel Littleton's shoulder. Rom
knew she was crying and a part of him ached for her tears
and wanted to comfort her, but he hardened his purpose
against the man who was his father and would not speak
for the sake of the woman—his mother.

Colonel Littleton patted her hair, awkwardly as men
will when they try to comfort their wives, and put an arm
about her and half-carried her to a chair. She had not
looked at Rom since she came into the room and she did
not look at him now, and the Colonel settled her in the
chair and turned to Rom and spoke again, harshly.

"Very well, Romulus Hormsby. I will, for my wife's
sake—and a little for my own, for I must know what you
carry in your mind—I will answer your question. Yet, I
cannot in truth answer it, for I never gave orders to anyone to rid me of my children, who were dearer to me than
anything else save only my honor."

"Do you deny . . ." Rom began. He was starting to feel
maybe Papa and Polly had been right about the letter. If
this were so what had he just done? He could not face the
thought and he began to beat it out of his mind with
bluster.

"Be quiet!" Colonel Littleton ordered with such deadly cold in his voice Rom obeyed. "I cannot answer so—so ridiculous an accusation. But you shall hear the full tale of my parting with my son and my daughter and of what thereafter befell and then you will answer *my* questions or I will have you beaten as you've never been beaten before."

"Bob, do not be harsh with the lad. He . . ."

"Leave be, Julia. I had for him nothing but thanks and good will when I came through yon door and he—he has given me insults in return. How would I *not* be harsh with him?"

"But, Bob . . ."

"*Julia!*" Colonel Littleton did not raise his voice but the single name commanded silence and she lifted her shoulders in patient acceptance and leaned against the padded chair and waited.

"Know you then, Romulus Hormsby, that in the year 1742 we were called by Charles Stuart, our rightful King, though denied his throne and banished from his kingdom, to come to him in France and to come with speed. I did not wait to settle my affairs, leaving them in the hands of my brother, Edmund, who was to sell my town house in Bath and my manor house and my lands and other possessions in the county and follow me as soon as my son and my daughter were recovered from the measles. We packed our belongings hurriedly, taking only such things as we needed, for we wished to travel fast and as secretly as possible. We even took four of the puppets—those you have seen here—for they had always been King Charles's delight. But we had no room for all of them and left the rest for my brother to bring to us later."

His face, which had been hard, softened when he mentioned his children and he looked briefly at his wife. She had covered her eyes and did not see the look and he went on.

"Romney and Mary were twins and when one was ill, so

must the other be. They were not fit to travel with us, but my King's summons had been urgent and I could not stay for their recovery. My wife, knowing their illness was only a mild one, would go with me since her presence too had been requested by our King. And so we left them with my brother, to come after us as soon as may be."

He stopped and closed his eyes and shook his head in a bewildered way and said, so softly Rom could hardly hear him, "We never saw them again," and gulped as if he found it hard to swallow and went on in a rush. "We searched. My brother had written, guardedly, of plans to visit some of King Charles's supporters to solicit funds for the Cause. He did not tell us which friends for fear his letter would fall into the hands of the false King. We sent messengers to all of them. None had seen him. We heard, time and again, reports of children found abandoned. We investigated them all and each of them with new hope and each time we were forced to suffer anew the agony of our loss. My brother and our children left Bath. So much we know. And disappeared. We have tried to put them out of our minds, to accept the knowledge that we will never see them again. And we had begun to accept, to build ourselves new lives in this new land. And now you come in mystery and stir the old pain. You shall not raise false hopes in us again, boy. You *shall* not. I will never again be led to believe my children live, for I am sure they cannot."

He went and stood above his wife's chair. She reached to take his hand and held it while minutes lengthened in silence broken only by the snapping of the apple logs in the great fireplace.

The fire had no power to warm Rom. His whole body ached with a cold that came from his heart. He must believe what he had heard and yet, if he believed it, how could he accept his own shame and willful stupidity? Pa—*Barney*—had tried to warn him and Polly had tried, and he had brushed their warnings aside, sure, in his pride, of his own judgments. He had accused Colonel Littleton, accused his father—almost accused him—of murdering his own children. How could he have been so wrong? He couldn't have been. He knew he couldn't.

The letter! Its orders surely were clear.

The thought of the letter brought him a last, thin hope that his own conduct was justified and he cried out into the quiet room, "But the letter! What of the letter?"

Colonel Littleton jerked up his head and Rom saw the traces of tears upon his face. "What letter?" he asked.

"'Your heart was ever stronger to rule your actions than your head. Despite your love and care you must be rid of them—both of them—and that right quickly. In these hard times there is no place for weak sentiment. What you must do, do quickly, and come straightly to us.'" Rom quoted the hated words as if they were before him and at the end, repeated slowly, "You—must—be—rid—of—them—both—of—them," and waited.

Robert Littleton shook his head in bewilderment and looked at his wife. She was out of the chair and staring at Rom as if she had, indeed, seen a spirit returned from the dead. "Do you know anything of such a letter, Julia?" Littleton asked, and she nodded, not turning to him, and spoke to Rom, "Who *are* you, boy?"

Rom did not hear her. "The *letter?*" he said.

"The letter," she repeated. "Did you think it was the children were to be got rid of?" She seemed to be in a kind of daze and spoke in a flat, low voice.

"Who else?" Rom asked belligerently, still fighting so that he need not admit his own fault.

"Horses," she said. "Favorite horses our brother Edmund wished to keep back when all else was sold. A pair of racing horses he had a fondness for, as he had always a fondness for animals. Nothing else. . . . Now will you tell us what you know of all this?"

Rom looked from the man to the woman and back again. "Oh, sir," he said, "oh, sir, what have I done to you and—and the lady? What . . . ?"

He felt tears begin to form behind his eyelids and thought he could not face these two in his shame and turned and ran from the room and from the house. He turned a corner and heard shouts and rounded a well-house and beyond it a dovecote and saw a narrow lane and took it and followed its twistings until he had left the town behind, and came to a recognized path into the forest. The sound of shouting was dim now and he stopped running and followed the path and found, at last, his secret place. He took the key from his pocket and got the door open and flung himself upon the dirt floor and lay there shivering in misery.

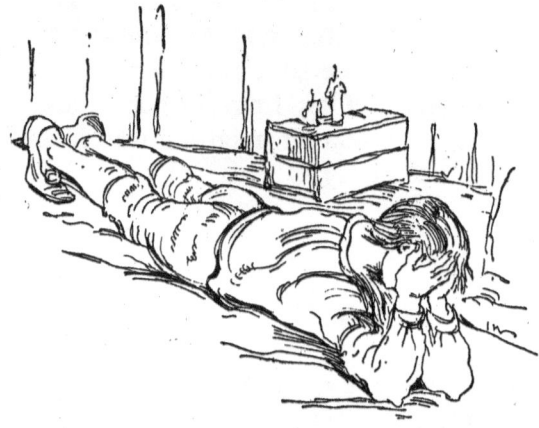

CHAPTER SEVENTEEN

Rom lay, forlorn, throughout the long hours of the afternoon while the sun became lost in gathering clouds that foretold more snow and the hut grew darker and colder. There were candle ends in a box he had brought against such a time of darkness and a fire was laid on the hearth beneath the smoke vent in the room, but he did not move to light the one or the other, hardly conscious of his own discomfort.

The same thoughts chased themselves about his mind. He had found his father and his mother and they were not monsters but kind and gentle folk who had suffered much: such a man and such a woman as he would have been proud to claim his own. He had found them and, with them, himself—his name, his roots, his identity. And in the very moment of finding he had lost again because his own stubborn pride had blinded him to the truth; because he would not wait to hear first what his father would say in excuse but had rushed blindly into accusations and cruel words that could not be recalled, and because he had not been willing to admit his mistake when first he had suspected it. He could never face them again. He would, in a little time, get up from this place and go away—away from his father and his mother, away from Barney and Polly and the Little People and his new-found joy in learning the art of acting. For all these things, too, were lost. In a little time.

He turned upon his face and buried his head in his arms and wished Polly were here to comfort him though he knew he did not deserve to be comforted.

Polly was at the tenement working with Mrs. Adcock upon the costumes for tomorrow's performance. It was a good day. The town was aglow with preparations for Christmas. The spicy smells of plum cakes and plum puddings and mince pies seemed to be one with the very air itself and she could still hear in her mind the sweet sounds of Christmas music from Bruton Parish Church where Mr. Pelham and the choir had been rehearsing as she passed.

She wondered how Rom was getting along with the scene he was preparing for Patrick Malone. Old Hallam had promised him a chance, on Twelfth-night, to test what he had learned so far. He was to have a real part, though a small one, in *The Beggar's Opera* when Pat would play the part of Mr. Peacham. This acting was good for Rom. He took to it naturally and it seemed to fill some kind of need in him. She glanced through the window of Mrs. Adcock's room and saw the sky darkening and hoped they would have a white Christmas.

"Where's Rom, Mistress Polly?"

Pat, able now to walk a little, asked the question. He had pushed open the door when no one had heard his quiet knock and he spoke around the opening.

"Is he not with you, Pat? He was working hard upon the scene you set him when I came away this morning. He planned to come to you later, as usual."

She was not especially concerned. No doubt Old Hallam had sent for him and he'd be along in a while. Or he had become so interested in what he was doing he had lost track of time.

Pat said good naturedly, "Drat the boy entirely," and took his head away and closed the door. Polly went back to her sewing and her own plans for the Christmas season and its days of merrymaking. The first lazy flakes of new snow drifted past the window. The fire flared as a log burned through. Polly and Mrs. Adcock sewed in friendly silence.

They heard the next knock, for it was furious, and they called "Come in" together and smiled at one another. The smiles faded quickly before the look on Old Hallam's face. He was clearly upset and worried and even before he spoke Polly felt his worry was for Rom.

"Where's your brother, Mistress Polly?" he asked.

"Indeed I couldn't say, Mr. Hallam." She thought, with a pang of worry, that if anything were wrong with Rom she did know where he was likely to be, but she would not tell Old Hallam or any other until she had learned what was amiss. "Is he not about the town, sir?"

"He is not. Unless he's found himself a cloak of invisibility. He is nowhere, and Bob Littleton sending his men —even Enoch Brown who never leaves his precious horses —running this way and that way and Bob himself coming to me and blathering—yes blathering, I say—about his long lost bairns he's not named since he came to Virginia in 1744—and making no sense about Rom and Rom's hidden knowledge of those same bairns . . ."

Polly heard his voice going on and on as if it came from a great distance but heard no words because her mind was caught in a great stillness. It seemed an eon of time, though it was, in truth no more than a second or two, before the stillness dissolved and she could think of what she had heard.

Two lost children and Rom with hidden knowledge of

184

them. Rom—somehow Rom must have discovered Colonel Littleton was their father and had—Dear Heaven! what would Rom have done? She knew too well his quick and unconsidering anger. What might he *not* have done had he come, unprepared, upon the knowledge that he had hated and dreaded to find and yet had half sought since Barney had told them their history? He might be in deep trouble. He might need help. Her cloak lay across a chair where she had dropped it when she came in. She flung it, any way, about her shoulders and bonnetless, forgetting Mrs. Adcock and Old Hallam, ran out into the quickening snow.

"What ails the girl?" Mrs. Adcock said, and Old Hallam echoed her, "What indeed?" and, after a moment, smiled to himself thinking Polly would find Rom if anyone could and added, "Let her be."

Polly ran through the town not seeing the curious stares that followed her. The curls that usually hung neat and careful over her shoulder bobbed and bounced and streamed out behind her, catching and holding the light, dry snowflakes. Her cloak swung crazily, half on, half off, and she clutched it about her with one hand.

She had to check her pace when she came to the forest ride that led to Rom's secret place, for the ground was rougher and her good sense told her she would be no help to Rom if she came to him with a twisted ankle or broken arm. Her mind seemed to move more slowly as she slowed her hurrying feet. When she could see the myrtleberry hedge through the snow she took time to make her curls neat again and straighten her cloak and force her look to cheerfulness.

The door was shut and no light showed through the cracks. Wasn't he there? Then she saw the iron padlock hanging open and pushed against the door and felt it give and peered into the gloom. She could see nothing and called "Rom?" and heard a sigh and whispered answer, "Polly, oh Polly."

185

She said, sharply, for she knew pity would be no aid to him, whatever he had done: "Get up, Rom, and make a light if you have candles. If you have none, I'll find a pine knot outside."

She heard vague rustlings in the half dark as he turned over and got up and groped to his cache of candle stumps and got one lighted. She almost cried out at sight of his face, tear-stained and marked with grief such as she'd not seen on it before. He was shivering and she took the candle from him and lit the dead leaves he had placed for kindling beneath the dry wood on the hearth. He came and stood beside her, his shoulder touching hers, and watched the fire get a small hold on the branches. After a moment he took her hand and she felt his fingers cold and stretched them, linked in hers, toward the little flame. When the warmth began to penetrate their bodies she sat upon the packed earth and drew him down beside her. "What is it, Rom?" she asked then. "What has happened?"

"I—I found—" he began and choked, wondering how he could tell her.

"Our father," she finished for him and he said, "You know?"

"I guessed, Rom. Was it—was it hard?"

He told her then—told it slowly and painfully, leaving nothing out to save himself in her eyes. When the telling was over he cried out to her, "What have I done, Polly? What have I done?"

She got up slowly and turned her back to the fire, feeling let down and more than a little foolish. I came to fight a lion, she thought, and have found, instead, only a small and frightened mouse. She said, "Nothing that can't be remedied and that right quickly."

He took his face from his hands and looked up at her and said, "What did you say?"

"I said you've done nothing that can't be put right quickly enough."

His mouth gaped at her in surprise. "You weren't listening," he said accusingly. "I said I had . . ."

"I *was* listening, Rom. I heard what you said and fully understood it. It is you who are not *thinking*. A few words spoken out of anger, a mind stubborn to keep its own mistaken sureness. Pooh! *I* feared you'd struck Colonel Littleton in your hating or—or done some other frightful thing. Words! Words can be explained away. Why must you always be making mountains from small hills, Rom? You did not use to be so. Do you think our—our true father and mother—especially if they are the kind of people you say they are—will remember harsh words or hold them against you when they know we are their own lost children? Do you begin to make some sense in your thinking, Rom Hormsby, and stop acting the child."

The candle end guttered and went out. The firelight showed Rom's eyes, unfocused, staring blank and straight at Polly though they did not see her. She waited until she could bear the waiting no longer and passed her hand in front of his face and said, "Rom!" sharply. He blinked his eyes and intelligence came into them again and he said, "Yes. Of course, you're right, Polly. Th—thank you for bringing some sense into my head. I—I was so—so shamed at my own prideful folly."

"Well, enough of it then. There's no time to waste in pitying yourself for your stupid mistakes. You're all rumpled and dirty and we must go back to the Widow Dawson's so you can make yourself decent. Yes, and we must take the ticket and the King Puppet, too, to Colonel Littleton, and the letter. And we must find Papa and tell him and get him to come with us."

She looked at the little flames which still burned low upon the hearth and thought they could not leave it so. "Come," she said, "we'd best get snow and put out the fire. No sense in letting this place burn down in our haste." She looked about the small room wondering if there were a vessel they could use for the snow. Rom, though he still had something of the look of the sleepwalker, went to a corner and found a broken jug and took it outside and filled it with snow and drowned the fire. Polly stirred the hissing ashes until she was sure there was no danger left and said, "Hurry," and they went out of the hut and locked it and made what haste they could back to the town.

It was late in the afternoon when Polly lifted the brass knocker on Colonel Littleton's door. She and Rom were alone, for when she had gone to the Printing Office to get Barney she found he'd ridden upon an errand to Yorktown and would not be back for some time and they had decided not to wait for his return.

The early winter dark shut out the street. Rom felt small and nervous and uncertain. He turned his woebegone face to Polly and she squeezed his hand and whispered, "Courage, Rom. All will be well. You'll see," but she wished someone would come to open the door for now they were here she was herself uncertain of their welcome.

She raised her hand to knock again and the door opened and a servant in black clothes stood in the square of light made by two candles in hurricane globes on a table in the hall behind him. He looked at them with a dignity he was far from feeling and waited, wondering who these two were and what they wanted. Whatever it was he'd best send them away. The Master was in a taking and the Mistress near sick with crying, and he'd not have them disturbed.

Polly shifted the bundle that held the Puppet King and waited for Rom to speak. He said nothing and she looked at him and saw him tranced and tongue-tied and knew she must do what was needful. She said, as politely as she could though her voice shook on the words, "We've come to see—to see—our—to see Colonel Littleton."

"Colonel Littleton's engaged. You not going to see him this night," the man in the door said, and began to close it.

Polly felt his hostility and did not know how to break

through it. "It—it is important we see him. Tonight," she said.

"I *said* the Colonel's engaged. If you got to see him you come back tomorrow. Colonel's been tried enough for one day. He tired out and resting. He . . ."

Polly interrupted, forgetting politeness. "He'll *want* to see us. What we have to say to him will help him, not hurt him more." She wondered if the servant would believe her if she told him exactly why they'd come and thought she'd best not risk telling him.

The man made no further effort to hide his exasperation. The day, he was thinking, had been a hard one for all connected with that house, with comings and goings and wailings and weepings, though what it was about nobody had bothered to tell him when they called him from his outside duties and bundled him into these fancy clothes to take old Sam's place while Sam went on some errand or another for the master. His patience was gone and he'd not waste any more time or any more words with two stubborn young ones, who were likely no more than trash though they looked gentle enough. He gestured Polly away, and started again to close the door.

Polly said, "Rom!" helplessly, and Rom came out of the fog that had bound his mind and moved. He looked at the man in the door and spoke sharply and with authority. "What's your name?"

"J—Job, s—sir," the man said, obviously startled by the authority in Rom's voice.

Rom snatched the bundle that held the Puppet King and put it into Job's hands. "Then, you Job, take that to Colonel Littleton and tell him Romulus Hormsby and his sister brought it," Rom said.

Polly had wrapped the Puppet King hurriedly in his royal robe with the Ankh embroidered upon it. As Rom thrust the bundle at Job the robe fell apart to show the puppet within. Job's eyes opened wider and wider and his mouth twisted in anger. He laid the bundle on a chair

189

and reached out and grabbed Polly with one hand and Rom with the other. They were too startled even to think what he was doing and before they could recover their wits he had yanked them inside and slammed the door and locked it and put the heavy key into the pocket of his striped waistcoat.

"You—you thieving buzzards," he said, spluttering. "You think I don't know what yon thing is?" He pointed to the Puppet King. "Just because I'm outside man don't mean I don't know the Colonel's little dolls when I see them. What you mean breaking in and stealing what Colonel Littleton think more of than he think of his eyeballs? Best I call the watch and send you to the jailhouse. Best . . ."

Polly saw the red flush rising in Rom's face and knew she must do something quickly. He'd be blustering in a minute and bluster wouldn't help them now. She made herself stand tall and straight and speak with a dignity and authority she didn't know she had. "Best you take the Puppet King and his robe to Colonel Littleton as you've been told and give him our message. You need not fear we'll run away. Even if you had not so discourteously locked the door upon us, it is not likely we would do so since we came freely asking for Colonel Littleton and freely offering what is not his but ours. Now go and lose no time."

Job was taken aback. His untrained mind could not cope quickly with her argument. But he knew authority when he heard it, yes, and quality, and he responded automatically to them. He hesitated still, but only briefly before he picked up the Puppet King and the robe and almost ran to the door through which small Amos had ushered Rom in the morning, leaving the twins standing forlornly in the cold hall beside the hurricane globes.

CHAPTER EIGHTEEN

Job knocked softly on the door of the library and waited and knocked again, a little harder. A voice, sounding tired and sad, bade him come in and he pushed open the door and crossed the room to the chair where Colonel Littleton sat staring into the fire. Job said, "Sir?" and looked quickly at the case which held the puppets and could not believe that each was in its accustomed place.

Colonel Littleton did not turn his eyes from the fire. "What is it, Job? Didn't Sam tell you I was not to be bothered?"

"He did do so, Colonel Littleton, sir," Job said, "and truth to say I hardly dast to bother you. But it was needful, Colonel, sir."

"Needful?"

"That it were, Colonel Littleton, sir. They'd not go away and they were thieving trash or—or seemed so—" he looked

again, doubtfully, at the case but it was still full—"and
I . . ."

"What are you talking about, Job?" Littleton turned his
head and saw the Puppet King and came out of his chair
in one movement. *"What is that?"*

"Like I'm telling you, Colonel, sir. It be one of your
little dolls. They thieving buzzards had it." He looked,
wildly now, from the puppet case to the King Puppet in
his hand and back again and wailed, "But Colonel, sir, it
gone and multiplied like they loaves and fishes! It do be
witched, sir, that it do."

"Nonsense, Job. The puppet you hold didn't come from
the case. It was lost long ago." In spite of an almost over-
powering impatience the Colonel took time to reassure
the badly frightened, superstitious Job. "Now, Job, give
me the bundle and begin again—at the beginning—and tell
me how you came by it."

Job practically dropped the Puppet King and the robe
in his eagerness to be rid of them. Colonel Littleton stared
at them, stroking first the puppet, then the robe.

"It was they thiev—the young lady and gentleman
brought it, Colonel, sir, and indeed I tried to send them
away not wishing them to be bothering you, but they
would not go and they—they made me bring yon things to
you and gave me a name to go with them but that I've
clean forgot."

"Where are they, Job? Where are they? You—you didn't
turn them out?"

Colonel Littleton placed the puppet and robe on the
table. His hands were shaking and he controlled his voice
with difficulty.

"Deed and I tried, Colonel, sir, but like I told you they
wouldn't anywise leave. They do be safe in the hall still."
Job took the key proudly from his pocket and held it up,
grinning at his own cunning, but Colonel Littleton was
no longer there to see it.

Two steps took him to the library door and he stood

there, seeing only the boy who had insulted him in his own library. Was that all to do over again, then? And what had the Puppet King, so long lost, to do with this Romulus Hormsby who had run away and hidden? His head was swimming and he closed his eyes to clear it. He became aware that the boy was talking. He must listen.

". . . how can I ask your forgiveness? How . . ."

Littleton held up his hand and said, "Wait!" The words sounded harsh and Rom's voice died and he wanted to run and remembered the locked door and knew he was trapped. He had been right in the first place. He should have gone far away from here. Gone and never come back. Why had he listened to Polly? His—his father would never forgive him and Rom could not blame him.

Colonel Littleton was breathing choppily with a dry, hard sound. For a while, there with the puppet in the library, he had dared hope, even believe, his children were not dead but alive and in Williamsburg. How else could anyone have come by the Puppet King? But here was only Romulus Hormsby again and no doubt he had, as Job thought, at some time stolen the puppets that had been lost. The Colonel managed to quiet his breathing and drive hope once more into its deep hiding place. But he could not speak with kindness to this boy who was so stubbornly set on keeping whatever information he might have to himself.

"Come into the library," he said harshly. "Did you not know I was seeking you? You owe me something in explanation of your behavior this morning and of how you come to be in possession of my property lost these ten years."

He turned and went back into the room. Rom did not at once follow and Polly, who had been hidden in the deeper shadows behind him, gave him a little push between the shoulders and whispered, "Go on, Rom."

"No," he said. "He'll never forgive me. You heard the sound of his anger. I'll *not* go."

"Of course you will, Rom." She giggled a little from nervousness. "You must, since we cannot leave by yon locked door. Let's get it over with."

"Romulus!" Colonel Littleton's call sounded menacing. "You've kept me waiting overlong already."

Polly took Rom's hand and half dragged him behind her. She stopped in the doorway and Littleton stared at her and said, "Who are *you?*"

"I—I think, s—sir," Polly said, trying to speak with the confidence that had all but left her, "I th—think we're your—your son and daughter, Rom and I."

Colonel Littleton's face turned quickly from white to red and back to white again. He caught the back of the chair beside him and Polly thought, dear heaven I've killed him for sure with the shock, and started toward him saying, "Oh, sir, I'm sorry. I shouldn't have spoken out so quickly like that."

He shook his head. "It—it—is nothing. It is only . . . *What do you mean, girl? What are you saying?* If this is your idea of a joke . . ."

Rom came from the doorway and put his arm about Polly's shoulders and said quickly and sternly, "There is no joke, sir." Now the words of identification were said, he was no longer nervous or uncertain. "We have come, sir, first that we might open to you the story of ourselves and second that I might, humbly, ask your pardon for—for doubts and for the words I spoke here this morning. Perhaps—perhaps, sir, if we all sat down, it would be easier."

Colonel Littleton, still white and shaking, eased himself into the chair he had been holding to. He stared at the two before him, trying to find in their faces some likeness to the babies he had left behind ten years ago. He could see no feature that was the same. He wanted to believe they were his, but he feared to believe and have his beliefs brought tumbling about him as had happened so often before. He would try to keep hope at bay until he had heard what they had to say. He would try. He said, "Sit down, then, and get on with your story."

194

Rom sat on a low stool beside the fire, but Polly went to stand at Colonel Littleton's side. It was she who began the tale they'd heard from Barney. Colonel Littleton listened with his head in his hands. When Rom laid the crumpled letter and the benefit ticket upon his knee he made no move to take them up or look at them.

Polly finished the account and looked at Rom. His head

was turned away from her and from Colonel Littleton. She wondered what was in his mind and felt bleak and lonely that she did not know and hated the sudden knowledge that they would be, increasingly as they grew older, thus separated in their thinking. She turned her look to the man in the chair and saw tears upon his face and put her hand timidly on his shoulder.

He moved then. He looked at her, unconscious, she thought, of his weeping, and reached up and covered her hand for a moment with his own. They are mine, he thought. The story is bound to be true. No one could imagine it. And they brought the Puppet King and his robe. "Mary," he said. "My daughter." He leaned a little forward and put his other hand on Rom's shoulder and gripped it hard. "Romney, my son."

Rom turned at his touch and got up from the stool and knelt beside his father. "Oh, sir," he said, "oh, sir, can you forgive the—the terrible things I said and—and the thought behind them? I—I am so ashamed."

"Hush, Romney Littleton. Between us three there need be no forgiveness—ever—only understanding. Had I been in your place I should have believed as you believed."

They were, then, robbed of words. Each was thinking his own thoughts. Each was full of his own emotion and a little embarrassed by this sudden new relationship. It was not easy to know what to say or even how to feel, for though they were father and children they were in truth strangers.

Rom moved first. "Than—thank you, sir," he whispered, and the whisper ran about the room and released them all from the spell of silence. Polly took her hand from Colonel Littleton's shoulder. Rom got off his knees and stood before the fire. And the Colonel came out of his chair calling, "Job! Sam! Amos! Fetch the mistress. Quickly."

The next minutes were full of confusion. Mistress Littleton, with old Sam and Job and young Amos, came running.

Her face, scored with the marks of old tears, was full of fear as she entered the library, looking at first to no one but her husband. Seeing him joyful, his arms stretched out to her in welcome, bewilderment chased away the fear and she stopped and looked about the room and saw Rom and Polly standing together and caught her breath. She looked again at her husband and back to the twins and gave a small cry and started toward them and stopped again and said, "Bob! Is it—It isn't . . ."

Colonel Littleton caught her about the waist and lifted her up as if she had been a child. "It is, Julia. It is they. They have brought the Puppet King and his robe and— and other things in proof."

She was away from him then and across the room so quickly she hardly seemed to move. She had the twins in her arms and even Rom forgot to be embarrassed and returned her hug and kiss.

A quarter of an hour later they were still marveling at the turn their lives had taken, with sentences begun and left unfinished, with ejaculations and interruptions and some tears and a great deal of laughter mixed all together, when Polly remembered Barney. "Papa!" she said, and Colonel Littleton said, "Yes, my daughter?" and Polly's face went red and she stammered a little, "No—no—sir. N—n—not y—y—you. Barney. I—he . . ."

"He's been Papa to us a long time, sir," Rom put in, seeing Polly distressed, "and we have given him no thought this hour past. May I go to him now, sir?"

"No, Romney," Mistress Littleton said gently, "let us rather send and bring him to us, for surely your father and I owe him more than any man living." She looked at her husband and he nodded and she went on, "Where is he, Romney?"

"Likely at the Widow Dawson's by now, ma'am," Rom said, wishing he could get his mind and his tongue to call her Mother.

Colonel Littleton said, "Job!" and Job came from the

door where, with old Sam and young Amos, he had been watching the reunion, still not sure what it was all about, though all of them had grinned until their faces ached. "Job, go along to the Widow Dawson's and fetch Mr. Barnabas Hormsby. Tell him nothing of what has happened here, but say Mistress Littleton and I have invited Master Rom and Mistress Polly to sup with us and would be honored if he would join our company. Do you understand?"

"Yes, sir, Colonel Littleton, sir. I do be on my way."

"And see no grass grows beneath your feet, Job."

"Not likely, Colonel, sir, with that snow coming down like the devil himself's blowing it," Job called back from the hallway.

While they were waiting Colonel Littleton told them more of his part of the story. They had gone to France, he said, he and his wife, to the court-in-exile of Prince Charles Stuart, for the Littleton family had always been royalists and worked secretly for the return of the Stuarts to the English throne. But, when all his searches for his children had failed to bring one single word of them, he had begged and been given leave by Prince Charles himself to take his distracted Julia to Virginia and here they had bought land and built a new life for themselves and prospered. And so, the Colonel said, he had been spared the final bitter defeat of his bonnie young prince on Culloden Moor.

"F—father," Rom said, trying on the word for the first time, "what of the ticket to Pat's benefit? Do you remember anything about it?"

"That I do, Romney. Your mother and I have always loved the playhouse. We and your uncle had been looking forward to the play"—he lifted the ticket from the table and flicked it with his fingers—"but it fair went out of our minds when the messenger came from Prince Charles. I believe it likely the ticket dropped into the puppet case, for your Uncle Edmund, who was our puppet guardian, was checking the rods when the messenger came. Likely it was just forgotten in the hurry that followed."

He paused, and looked into the fire and added slowly, after a moment, "Would your uncle had taken the road to Plymouth, as we had planned, when he started with you two to join us. What caused him to carry you right across England? He was, evidently, planning to take ship from Dover or Portsmouth. No wonder we could get no word of you, for all our searches centered upon Bath and Plymouth. Why, I wonder, *why* did he shift his course without letting us know?"

Julia Littleton put her hand on his arm. "It is useless to wonder, Bob," she said gently. "Thank God—and Barnabas Hormsby—we'll have the rest of our lives for catching up with our children, and for wondering what happened those ten years ago."

CHAPTER NINETEEN

Rom stood in a shadowed corner of the stage waiting for the play to begin. All about him the bustle of the final preparations for *The Beggar's Opera* was making a bedlam of the stage; but he was shut away from the confusion, alone with his own nervousness.

This, he thought, was Twelfth-night—the time he'd been looking forward to for weeks, working toward for weeks, the time when he would make his first real appearance as an actor with lines in the Hallam Company. He should be proud and glad. Instead his knees and hands were shaking, and his skin, beneath his beggar's costume, was damp and cold. He was certain he'd forget his lines, or stumble awkwardly about the stage, or enter or exit at the wrong time, or do some other stupid thing that would ruin the whole play. He told himself again and again that what he might do or fail to do could not matter because his part was so small. It did no whit of good.

He felt the same kind of panic he'd known when Rafe had tried to upset him as he spoke the lines of the prologue and he knew he must, somehow, turn his mind away from tonight's show before he took to his heels and ran out of the Playhouse. Deliberately he set his mind upon reliving scenes from the last three weeks, reliving them as if they were going on here and now.

It was, again, the day they found their father and mother. They were waiting for Barney and when he was announced with a great flourish by Job, Barnabas Hormsby took one look at their happy faces and needed no telling of what had happened. Everyone talked at once and when, at last, all the stories and starts of stories came together in one sensible explanation, the Colonel asked Barney to leave his work at the Printing Office and become a part of the Littleton household. Barney shook his head slowly. "Indeed, sir," he said, "I thank you with my whole heart. But you see, Colonel Littleton, here's the truth of it. I've never been one to sit around and do nothing."

Colonel Littleton started to interrupt, and Barney held up his hand. "If it please you, sir, I'll just finish my say. I'm doing what I like and what I know best how to do. And there's the Widow Dawson besides. It's hard for a lone woman, sir. There's many a way I can help her and it's a good feeling to know you're helpful. No, sir, I'll stay on as I am, only, with your permission, I'll come often to visit the Littleton family for I'll always feel the bairns are part my own."

They went, he and Polly, toward Barney as if they were moved by a single puppet master. Their faces showed the shock they felt at his words. "Then we'll stay with you, Papa," they said together.

Barney put an arm about each of them and held them close to him. "That you'll not, bairns," he said. "You've been my trust and my happiness these ten years, as close to me as if you'd been in truth my own flesh and my own blood. But you belong with your own true parents and I—if I were to follow you as the Colonel so kindly offers, I'd be again like that same Othello—without an occupation. No, it's best this way—my way, and I'll have no grieving. I've a place in this town of Williamsburg and work to do, and I like it so. And I'll likely see you each day."

Polly began to cry and Rom to argue, but Barney stopped them with his old to-be-obeyed voice. "Do you be quiet, Romulus and Polly. It's so I want it. It's so it will be, and we'll say no more about it but set ourselves to rejoicing with the Colonel and his lady that what they had lost is found at last, and that right joyfully."

Christmas Day. Christmas was, here in Williamsburg, a quiet day, a day more religious than secular in its keeping except for a very feast of a dinner. Rom and Polly, dressed in fine new clothes went to Bruton Parish Church with Barney and their new-found parents. Polly preened herself a little when, after the long Christmas sermon, she and Rom were taken around and introduced to family friends. And that, Rom thought, feeling shy and uncomfortable among the gentlemen and their fine ladies from all over the Colony, seemed to mean the whole churchyard-full of folk. He was much happier when dinner was over and the curtains in the Littleton house were drawn and the family, alone together, gathered in the twilight about the spinet and sang Christmas carols. Later they brought out the Little People—the Hormsby puppets rejoined now to those others made so long a time ago—and gave a puppet play about the Nativity.

The following day in his father's library. "Barney tells me, Romney," his father said, "that your schooling has been sound, that you can construe Latin easily and have already a little Greek and can do sums passably. In truth, from what he tells me, I am sure you are nearly ready for the College, where you can begin studies that will fit you to handle the estates that will be yours and take your proper place in the affairs of this country. Perhaps, later, you would like to go back to England and . . . what is it, Rom? What troubles you in this?"

Rom did not know he was frowning. "F-f-father," he said, "I— Did you not know I am a member of the Hallam Company? That is why I have gone each day to work with Patrick Malone, so that I may become a better and better actor. I—I have no wish to go to the College—or—or to—to do these things you speak of. I—I am going to be an actor, and Mr. Hallam says I can learn to be a good one, he is sure."

He was, for a moment there in the quiet room, afraid of his father. Colonel Littleton's face seemed to swell as blood rushed into it. He clenched his hands over the arms of his chair and half rose from it. Rom took a step away from him and Colonel Littleton saw upon his son's face the look that had been there when Rom had first come into this library. Slowly, Colonel Littleton assumed his accustomed look of kindness. He sat back again and his hands relaxed. "Forgive me, son," he said. "Your Mother and I had hoped you would be content to stay here with us now that we have, at last, found you. I had hoped you would become a planter and a citizen of this growing land. But it is, I suppose, natural that you would rather stay in the kind of life you have come to know best. And I'll not force you. You must make your own choice. I only ask you to give the matter serious thought."

The day his father took him to Littleton Plantation overlooking the river. They went from room to room in the graceful brick house that stood on the bluff above the broad, blue water. He had never before seen a house so richly furnished and yet so like a home. Later they went to the stables and his father told him to take his choice of horses. "For my own?" he asked, and his father said, "They are all yours, Rom, yours and Polly's, for everything your mother and I possess is held as a trust for the two of you. But I thought likely you'd want to choose the horse you'd prefer to ride on most occasions."

They spent the afternoon riding over the fields that belonged to the house. His father explained how tobacco was grown and cut and cured and stored and spoke of experiments he was planning with crops that would be less greedy for new land than the tobacco, which wore out the soil. The fields seemed to call Rom and he wondered what it would be like to spend all of his days moving with the earth from seedtime to harvest.

"Rom!"

Rom jumped at Patrick Malone's call. Patrick sounded relieved. "Whatever are you doing here by yourself, hiding in a corner? Hallam's pulling his hair out, wondering where you are. We're about to begin."

He hustled Rom to the wings, and before he could begin to panic again, Rom was on the stage and through his lines without mishap and standing to one side while the opera swept on around him.

He was, then, an actor!

He should be feeling proud or—at least—pleased with himself and his new role. He had proved himself as a member of the Company. There had even been a round of applause from the audience for his acting. He could see Old Hallam grinning in the wings, and Patrick had given him a wink as he finished the chief part of his role. He should be looking forward to his next play, hoping Old Hallam would give him a bigger part. He should be filled up with excitement, as he had expected to be if he could just get through this first test.

But he wasn't. He was in no way moved. Instead of

thinking about these things he was remembering what Pat had told him while they were getting into their costumes. "You know, Rom, we'll be moving on before long. Hallam thinks we'll likely stay here a while longer, then go up to the Northern Colonies, try our luck in New York or Philadelphia."

Rom had been too busy to pay much attention to Pat at the time, but now the memory of the words made him feel desolate and forlorn. A month ago he would have run whooping in pleasure with the news to Barney and Polly. Now . . . ?

He had not thought much about an actor's life. He had been content to find that he belonged to a close-knit group, to find a kind of family when he had been bereft of his own. He had not realized that being an actor would mean settling in one place, getting to like it and the people in it, and then, just when you were feeling permanent again, having to move on and do the whole thing all over again in a new town. He thought of the plantation and wondered when the first tobacco seeds would be dropped into the sheltered beds his father had shown him. He wondered how Remus would run in the spring race. The horse hadn't been entered as planned in the December running because Enoch Brown thought it best to give him more time to get over being stolen and painted and hidden away. Enoch would let him ride in that race, he was sure—ride all out to win this time.

He thought of the guitar and the German flute his father had bought for Polly and himself and the lessons they were taking learning their new instruments. Polly would go on, in quiet summer evenings, playing the guitar while their mother brought the old tunes from the spinet and their father made his violin sing. But Rom would not be with them. He wanted to be with them. He wanted to come home in the late afternoon from a day riding about their own place upon his own horse he'd named Romulus and, bathed and refreshed, watch the sunset over the river.

205

Well, he thought, nobody can have everything. Whatever you choose must be paid for in some coin. He had chosen to be an actor and he reckoned he could have a good life on the stage. But he didn't, in his heart, believe it.

He looked toward the box where Polly sat with their father and their mother and, behind them, Barney. And, as he watched them, the whole meaning of his new life was made plain. He knew he had not merely changed one name for another, one way of living for another. He knew his heart and mind were no longer restless. He had a name that was truly his own. He had, again, the security he had lost half-a-year ago in a sun-filled tobacco barn in a strange land. He had a place where he belonged. He had come home, not indeed to a loved and familiar house, but to an ordered and anchored way of thinking and feeling.

And suddenly he knew he would not leave it again. He had thought he wanted to be an actor above all things. Each day he had worked with Pat he had grown more skilled and more eager to improve his art. This, he had thought, was what he wanted more than anything in life. Now he knew he had only been looking for something to fill the lonely places within him. What was it Old Will Shakespeare had said? "All the world's a stage, and all the men and women merely players." Well, this would be his world, this Virginia would be his stage. He would tell Old Hallam as soon as the play was done. Tell him and thank him and then tell his father and watch the slow smile spread over his father's face and his mother's eyes shine again, the sadness that had been in them gone forever.

He saw Polly leaning forward and knew she had stopped watching the play and was concentrating on him. He made a small sign with his hand, their special sign that all was well, and thought, she knows I'll be staying and she's glad.

He said, inside himself, "Romney Littleton, Virginia gentleman," and he liked the sound of the words.

www.ingramcontent.com/pod-product-compliance
Lightning Source LLC
Chambersburg PA
CBHW030324020726
47493CB00004B/1149